STEVE

By

D.R. Webb

'It's all about the music'

COPYRIGHT

SUPPORT

This book addresses some adult themes around homelessness, mental health, substance and physical abuse.

The author does not endorse any negative activity that can impact a person's wellbeing, physically or mentally. Although all characters in this publication are fictitious and any resemblance to real persons, living or dead, is purely coincidental. The author has been personally impacted by some of the themes in this work of fiction. As such he takes the issues in this work very seriously and therefore has decided to try help combat the issues raised in this novel.

A portion of the eBook royalties will be donated to charity more information on: www.drwebb.co.uk

For additional Support please contact:
www.shelter.org.uk
ww.mind.org.uk
www.samaritans.org
www.actiononaddiction.org.uk

INSPIRATION

Families come in all shapes and sizes, they are the people that have your back, they are the people that love you unconditionally. But not all family is blood.

Family can be created by lost souls finding each other, from a stranger's light illuminating your darkened path.

Forget the simplicity of hatred and pain.

Do the harder thing and love one another.

Only then will you reap the rewards!

PROLOGUE

The acrid stench of urine filled the dimly lit room. The wind battering the side of the house sounded like a deranged creature trying to claw its way inside. The smashed windowpane allowed the bitter wind in to stir up the stench even more.

The dilapidated space was dripping with rain and despair. There was no light being emitted from the eroded light fittings, and the darkness hid creatures that scurried along the edge of the room. In the middle of the floor was a stained mattress; atop it lay a sleeping woman.

Around her sleeping frame the wallpaper loomed forward as it peeled downward. From the walls, the plaster had separated, leaving exposed wooden splines beneath, like bones poking through a corpse. On the ceiling above her unconscious body, graffiti covered every inch of the remaining plaster.

She let out a quiet snore and her nose wrinkled. The acrid stench of stale alcohol and urine crept upon her. Still, she slept.

The mattress on which she lay was heavily stained with the sides torn. The down filling poked out from the side, intertwined with sharp, rusted springs.

Breaking the soundtrack between the wind and the eerie silence was a creak from the only door to the room. The sound was loud and piercing in the room, but it did not disturb her slumber. Through the door an older man in his fifties entered the room. His hair was scruffy, unkempt, with white and grey matted together. It was not dissimilar to a bird's nest, resting above his aged face.

His eyes darted over to the sleeping woman, the eyes, sunken, grey, and dark, fixed upon her. He creeped quietly over and reached out his gnarled and dirty hand to her; his nails were blacked with soil and filth.

He stopped over the woman and took in her beauty. She was equally filthy, but her beauty shone through the grime. Her hair was greasy but bunched neatly down by her ear and her skin was marked with bruises and dried mud.

He cast his eyes down past her face to her hand and settled on a wrap of wire around her ring finger. It was the only jewellery that adorned her thin raggedy body. He took another silent step towards her; his black dress shoes were riddled with holes. His next delicate step caused the floor to creak under him. Still, she did not wake.

Using his hand on his knee to ease himself down he lowered himself to her and leered over her. He moved his hand from his dirt encrusted jeans and placed it tenderly on her shoulder, caressing her arm gently before tightening his grip.

He shook her gently, "Mandy!", he cooed barely louder than a whisper. "Mandy, wake up!"

She began to stir; in the near distance a clatter brought her to a start. Her eyes opened wide as she bolted and sat upright. The man put his finger to his lip signalling her to be quiet. "Shhh! We have got to go!" He whispered; the urgency hidden by a falsetto emulating calm.

"What, now!?" Mandy asked, stretching her arms wide as she spoke.

"Yeah, right now, just get together what you can carry, and do it quickly!" he spoke in hushed tones, but the urgency struck her.

She jumped up off the mattress and started pulling on her trainers. She shuddered as she pulled on the first one, because it still felt damp. She took the other in her hand and wiped off a little of the partially dried mud on the filthy mattress before resigning herself to force the second one onto her feet. There was a banging noise coming from somewhere within the building; Mandy could not quite work out where it was coming from, the only thing she knew was that it was getting closer and getting louder. The man was flurrying around the room, being careful not to make a noise, gathering up odds and ends that were scattered around, throwing them into a damp looking backpack.

Mandy had at this point gathered herself together and was standing in her tattered yellow, wool lined coat, holding a bag over her shoulder. The man stopped moving and looked around the room, His lips moving as if he was mentally taking check, mouthing out the list of essentials in his mind. An explosion of noise turned both of their heads towards the door. It was still closed. Under the door, beams of light could be seen darting back and forth.

They looked towards each other, their eyes met,

he grabbed her hand and led her to the window. The empty window-frame leaving a hollow escape route into the darkness of night. The man gently helped her slide out past the windowsill then grabbed her hands, lowering her tenderly to safety before he released her. She fell the short distance to the floor and stood up immediately. As soon as he saw she was safely on the ground, he immediately threw out the backpack from the floor next to him.

He turned on his heels and crawled backwards out into the bleak darkness below. He dangled for a moment, holding onto the ledge before dropping hard onto the floor. He rolled as he landed from the upper floor, luckily the grass was wet and over-grown, providing a little padding. He was an older man, but he was nimble enough.

As he hit the ground, the sound of the old wooden door slamming open exploded from the room above them. He picked up his backpack and took Mandy by the hand before bolting into the night. There was overgrown bushes and vegetation acting as accomplices to their escape, easily hiding their path and direction from anyone wishing to follow.

They ran into the night until even the tight grip he had on her hand was not enough to force her to keep up with him, she fell behind and pulled free.

She doubled over panting loudly, "I need to stop for a minute". Slowly, she re-gained her breath, finally standing straight she looked at him, "What the hell was that about?"

The man looked behind them, there was consid-erable distance between the dilapidated old home and them now. "Security" he gruffly offered. "I was keeping watch while you slept, they saw me with their god damn flashlights".

"I knew it was a mistake to break into that derelict house on that new development plot" She shook her head as she spoke.

"Well, those two security lads certainly would agree with you. I just wanted to get you out the rain for a night. You were soaked to the bone." He offered sweetly as he stepped towards her raising his hand to stroke her face.

"Steve, Stop!" She said taking a step backwards.

"How many more times are we going to do this?" she cried out, tears filling her eyes.

"It's just till were on back on our feet".

"You've been saying that for five years Steve, and I don't know if I can do this anymore". Tears still rolled silently down her cheeks.

"Come-on baby, don't you trust me anymore?" he asked, a hint of desperation in his voice.

"I just don't think I can do all this running round anymore, I'm tired of doing this, we're too old for this, I'm too old for it".

Steve stepped forward to her and wiped her tears away, which she allowed. He rested his hands in her hair and kissed her, "let's just get to the city, I'll find some work, everything will be better, I promise".

"But you've been saying that for years".

His lips curl into a warm smile before he spoke, "This time!" he offers. His hand took hers and guided her gently forward. She dropped her reluctance and effortlessly followed him into the moonlit night, disappearing into the darkness together.

CONTENTS

CHAPTER ONE

November blows in a new cold air, the school is displaying a mass exodus of children. Joyful cheers ring out a call that screams the day is done. They flee from the grounds, laughing, running, and playing. As the crowd thins out, a lone boy slowly walks into the bitter wind.

His jumper is torn, and backpack is threadbare, he is lost in his own thoughts and makes no effort to acknowledge any of the other straggling children.

The double doors of the school fly open menacingly, a stern looking man steps out into the low afternoon sunlight. He is dressed in a black knitted jumper atop a blue shirt, he exudes authority even in just the power of his stance.

"Kase!" he calls out causing the boy to turn.

"Don't forget your homework tomorrow, I won't accept excuses again." He doesn't wait for a response before disappearing back into the dreary stone building.

The boy turns back towards the gates and moves slowly towards them. He kicks at the ground with each step as if angry with the very ground conveying him forwards. Finally, as with all journeys he reaches his destination. It is an austere looking house, doused in grey pebble dashing. Low sunken windows adorn this grim homestead. The rotting wood of the window frames aging the property further.

The entire row of terrace houses looked like a jilted remnant of an abandoned town. There was no garden but ironically a garden gate rusted and jagged leading onto a thin strip of mossy, cracked paving slabs. He arrives at the door reaching into his pocket retrieving a small silver key. The door creaks open and the wood covering the smashed glass panels at the top groans with the movement.

He closes it and walks swiftly upstairs into his room, easing himself onto his unmade single bed. His room is quite bare, mould is creeping its way down the wall from the ceiling. He lays down on the bed wincing as he moves, his ribs aching and throbbing, but he pays it no mind, just closing his eyes.

***

The alarm clock on the floor ticks steadily on, the hands on the face read 2:17. The screaming downstairs is penetrating the room through the floor. The sound gets louder as the young lad's eyes open. This was the third time this week alone. He was now fully awake, but made no effort to move from the bed.

Glass shattered below him followed by a loud shrill scream. A man's voice became louder, he could now hear each obscene word that was being thrown by his father. His mother could be heard sobbing before another crash broke the affray causing another shrill scream to escape the woman.

Deeper in the house a door slammed open and a booted foot slammed down on the stairs. Another stomp. Another stomp. Tears filled the boy's eyes as he lay motionless. Another stomp. For a moment, the house became eerily quiet, the boy held his breath as the tears silently rolled down his face.

The doorknob emitted a squeak, yet the door remained still. His moist eyes remained focused on the ceiling not daring to move. There was silence for the longest time before a footstep broke the quiet, flanking off into another room slamming the door. The boy exhaled and closed his eyes, trying to block out the darkness in the house but his attempt was in vain.

The tight feeling of panic in his chest reached a crescendo when an explosion of noise erupted from downstairs. It sounded like wood and metal crashing together. Like a car had driven headfirst into the property. The boy bolted upright because as much as he had become accustomed to the noise of fighting and things breaking, this was a foreign sound to him. Some new unknown terror.

Pounding footsteps could be heard echoing all over the house, downstairs, on the stairs, in the hallway. The army of footsteps, parading the house introduced a new sound. "POLICE!" The boy climbed down from the bed and slipped underneath, trying to put a shield between the new terror and himself.

Within seconds the door to his room burst open and the sight of a police officer dressed in stern black uniform stood observing the dimly lit room. The man had a smartly trimmed beard and piercing blue eyes. He had a matt black gun pointed down at the floor as he called in, "POLICE, Show yourself".

The boy shivered as fear took hold of him, he was unable to move or respond to the commands and just tried to shrink into the darkness under the bed. In the hallway, the boy saw another two officers, dressed in the same neat uniform. This time they had a handcuffed man between them, guiding him down the stairs. The lad recognised his father in the handcuffs, his unkempt shoulder length hair matted with blood which also coated his face.

He was barely conscious, and his head was lolling from one side to the other as he slurred obscenities at the officers, "YOU COCK!!, FUCK YOU!!, FUCKING PIG!!".

The boy watched on as the officer in the doorway turned his attention back to the room. He walked forward shining his flashlight around the bare room.

Another officer joined him and moments later the bed was lifted off into the air and the boy was exposed.

Still in his school uniform he lay crouched trembling in fear, and even as the officer picked him up and carried him outside, he still felt a deep terror. The officer was kind and sat with him in reassuring silence until a social worker arrived. The pair helped him into a car and together, they set off towards the emergency room to have him examined.

***

Kase was laying in the bed of his foster home, his eyes looking up to the celling, his mind reliving that night as he often did. Sleep fleeing from him like an uncatchable foe. He remembers getting carried from his family home. It was a violent home, it was a dilapidated home, it was an abusive home, but for 9 years of his life, it was the only home he knew.

The rest of the night becomes a bit of a blur reduced to words he keeps slowly repeating. He remembers being put into a police car and the officer waiting with him 'CAR'. He remembers a social worker sitting with him and asking questions to which he had no answer 'CANT'. He remembers the blood everywhere 'RED'. He remembers the sound the social worker made when the doctor examined him, all the bruises, the broken ribs 'PAIN'.

"CAR"
"CANT"
"RED"
"PAIN"

He slowly repeats them, even in his dreams he hears these words.

***

Kase has had a rough journey since that night six years ago. His first meeting with the social worker was hard. He was taken for an examination at the hospital, the doctor there was kind but unfamiliar. The social worker, Anne, was nice enough but was fairly cold; the only time she made any indication she was actually human was when he had to remove his top to be examined.

The purple and red bruises ran throughout his body from the beatings and his Xray showed that bones had been broken and healed, many times over. After he was done with the doctor Anne took him to his first foster home. They were a nice couple that had no other children in the house. They were kind to him, but sadly he was not able to stay there. Anne showed up one day out the blue and grabbed all his possessions and without so much as a goodbye, he was gone onto the next foster home.

He was 16 now, but still looked incredibly young, his face was still quite childlike in many ways, even the fuzz around his top lip was barely visible. He had lived in several different foster homes, some homes were nice, most were less so. Some hit, some didn't give enough food, some got too 'close'. Anne had through his life become the harbinger of change.

Months would pass where he didn't see her, then one day she would show up out the blue and tear him out of the home, school, friendships. Hope felt more like an unachievable buzzword, like happy or free, something for others, not for himself. He was steadily approaching his 17th birthday, only a few months before he got a step closer to freedom.

His current foster home was manageable. The adults didn't really speak to him, and they didn't really feed well. They even put a lock on the fridge after he helped himself to some extra food. Mostly, they had no expectations. He went from school to his room and then to sleep. It was a merge existence but at least he was free from harm. School was something that he struggled with, he was heavily dyslexic and struggled to read.

He never got the chance to get any support to build his literacy as he moved around so much. He was ashamed of his inability to read or write, he preferred to be known as the naughty foster kid than try and be known as the stupid kid that nobody wanted.

He was sat at on the floor of his bedroom looking at his homework, it was a simple worksheet from a year many under his own teaching group. It had mathematical problems on it. He tried to read the first line.

ßàœ€ Î¥€Uȝ ƛժȒȝժ ∩ȞSFȜ ΨხƄÝϚσyź ъщ 4 ж 2 ⊦ ?

He scrunched his eyes and rubbed his temple. "Why is it so complicated, why am I so fucking stupid?" he asked himself. The questions kept circling his mind, he tried to look again but the letters had all moved around making even less sense. He took his pen but hesitated, deciding to scrunch the paper up and throw it balled-up back into his backpack uncompleted.

He climbed into bed, frustration causing his eyes to tear up he covered his eyes and tried to sleep. He longed to escape it all. 'CAR'. He wished his stomach would not make such noises, hunger was an old friend of his now, it was just another thing he couldn't control. 'CANT'. He heard footsteps coming from the hall, the door to the room opened, creaking slightly as it did. His foster dad stood at the door. He did not speak, nor did he leave. 'RED'.

Kase didn't move, that familiar feeling of fear was washing over him, fear mixed with the acrid stench of alcohol. The man slowly, menacingly, walked over to the boy. He heard something drop to the floor then something touched his face. He knew from his last home the routine by now. If he pretended to be asleep and it was easier, when he tried to fight, they were sadistic and purposefully made him suffer. 'PAIN'.

Kase kept his eyes scrunched up until he drifted off into a very disturbed nightmare. He was in a cage surrounded by bars made of words. These ones he could read clearly. There were the four that haunted him and other like; VICTIM, SUFFER, DESERVED, PUNISHMENT, TRAPPED, UNWANTED. Outside of the cage was a doorway, beautifully lit in light blue and teal, on the floor was a rug leading through the door with the word FREEDOM.

This was the recurring nightmare he hated the most. Not only was he caged in his waking life but in his dreams too. He felt a new feeling rise in him, it rose in his chest, it scorched him like fire. He felt his oesophagus burn as if magma was lining his stomach and an eruption was coming. His feet felt the heat first and this feeling rose in him until he felt it in his head.

He woke from his nightmare alone in his room. This new feeling still powerfully burning him. His hand reached towards his face and wiped off the sticky, crusty residue. With it he wiped away the shame, but not the heat. The new sensation he felt, he finally identified, was rage. The room was dark, his foster dad had turned the lights off as he left the room. There was a low glow in the room from the streetlights outside. He looked at the clock, the hands pointed at 10:45pm. He paced in the room for a minute, his mind racing from his newfound emotion.

He finally had a goal, an objective. He would finally break the bars of the words that imprisoned him. He would be free from the cage of words that imprisoned his dreams. He would escape.

He sat on the edge of the bed and reached for his backpack. He scooped out the folders and paper sheets discarding them on the bed, they were now remnants of a life he was leaving behind.

His backpack now empty he grabbed his only non-school clothes from the drawer next to the bed. In his hand he held a pair of jeans that were a little too loose kept up by a sturdy leather belt, a plain black t-shirt, underwear and socks. He put them in his backpack and made his way to the bathroom, stopping only to take a singular picture of his mother from under the mattress. He showered thoroughly to wash the filth off his young face and dried himself quickly.

Once he was changed, he discarded the uniform in the bag and carried it downstairs to the front door. He put on a hoodie and a beautiful three-quarter length black wool coat that belonged to the foster dad, finishing off the look with a blue and black knitted scarf.

Now wrapped for the journey, he knew he needed money. They always kept their wallet and purse in a locked drawer by the front door. The key would be in their room, he pondered for a moment, but he realised it wasn't worth the risk of being caught, of them learning his plan too soon.

He quietly crept to their beautiful kitchen. When he first arrived, he noticed the beach-coloured doors and marble counters that created a grand appearance to the room. He had never seen a kitchen so beautiful, not that he was allowed in it, yet another place he was forbidden to enter, not tonight he thought. He reached into a drawer in the island and retrieved a long screwdriver to pry the drawer open with. The drawer offered overall extraordinarily little resistance, opening with a quiet pop.

Even the little sound made Kase freeze, amplified by the silence of the residence. After a few seconds hearing nobody stir he rifled through it, searching for valuables. Car Keys, "no! that won't do" he pondered. "Ah, his wallet", smooth black leather, monogrammed with his foster dad's name on the lower left panel.

Kase opened it, slightly disappointed at the mere £40 inside. He took it, along with a debit card and ID. He didn't know if he would be able to use it, but he didn't want him to have it, smirking at the patty revenge. He looked at the purse and took the notes from that too, £120 not too bad. He pocketed the notes and some jewellery he found, a gold ring &

silver bracelet.

He clicked the drawer closed again and swiftly crept to the kitchen screwdriver in hand. He got to the refrigerator and looked at the lock bolted to the front of it, he pondered for a minute, "why would the social worker not pick up on that?". He tried to pry the lock open, and it clunked loudly, causing him to stop immediately and listen for movement.

Footsteps could be heard above him, moving around. He froze, fear washing him of his bravado. Footsteps continued above him and walked to the hallway above, his eyes widened, would he be discovered? As the stairs started to creak, he ran to the back door, the way to the front now blocked. At the back door he reached to handle and to his horror the keys were missing.

Eyes darting around he fixed on the utility room, he sprinted in as quietly as he could muster. Hiding behind the door he tried to block out all noise, even his breathing seemed to pause. His hands shook as they brandished the screwdriver. The lights in the kitchen flickered to life and somebody stumbled around the kitchen. More sounds assaulted Kase's tender nerves.

Water, steps, kettle, steps, steam whistling, steps. He sees a shadow scope past the gap under the door, his hands grasp even tighter on the screwdriver. One way or another he was leaving that house tonight. He hears keys jingling and a teaspoon clattering against a cup. Suddenly, the light vanishes from under the door and silence floods the room.

He cowers in the room a little longer, not sure if he dares open the portal from perceived safety to impending danger. Footsteps can be heard again in the bedroom above; he could put it off no longer. He digs into his will and twists the door handle and peers into the kitchen. It is empty.

He had almost resigned himself to leaving the house with nothing more than the blanket he found in the laundry room, when he noticed the milk bottle, left on the counter, next to it lay an open padlock. He swept his eyes over to the fridge which was indeed left unlocked. He pulled his backpack open and threw into the bin his mono-grammed school uniform top and jumper, keeping only the trousers.

Into the bag he also threw some food from the fridge, some cans from the cupboard, breakfast bars, fruit, and crisps. His mind raced, he was nearly free. He was scared to run away, but not as much as he was to stay. Before closing the bag, he slid the screwdriver inside, enjoying the feeling of not being so defenceless for once.

He put the milk away and closed the fridge, locking it as he walked from the kitchen, towards his freedom. He arrived at the front door, his hand rested on the handle, his other on the key. He breathed in his last breath of imprisonment and in one swift, decisive motion he turned the key, pulled the handle down and sprints out into the darkness. Not once did he look back, the evil cold wind felt more like a caress of an invisible deity beckoning him forward into freedom.

***

Kase arrived at the train station and approached the information desk, which was unmanned. He frantically started looking for anyone to help him, but nobody materialised. The sight of a timetable mounted on a nearby wall drew his eye. It was no good, he couldn't read it.

As he stood there, panic rising in his chest again, he overhead a man behind him talking on the phone. "Yeah, it's in forty minutes, are you meeting me at the station when I get to the city?"

He climbed the stairs to the platform behind the man and took a seat, this was the first time the sting of the cold started to permeate his bones.

Was this a mistake? Was it too late? NO! He was free, and he was going to live free from now on! Minutes passed quickly, his eyes darting to the platform entrance, he couldn't be stopped now, he was too close. A few people littered the platform, and although nobody paid him any attention, he couldn't help but feel nervous.

Finally, an announcement rang through the platform; "The next train to arrive will be on platform two, in five minutes, this train is on time".

Kase tapped his foot rapidly, even as the train pulled into the station slowly grinding to a halt. He stood up and rapidly boarded the train as the doors closed behind him.

He took a seat in the carriage and started to take in his surroundings; gum was mounted to the back of the chair ahead of him and graffiti was scribbled over the carriage wall. As the train began to slowly pull away, he mouthed out "on to a new start".

The guardsman was a large gruff looking man, with a portly stomach and a bald, shiny head. The buttons of his shirt looked to be struggling to stay closed, and if they were sentient the buttons would have groaned under the strain. He bobbled down the carriage calling for tickets even though as far as he was aware he was the only new customer in that part of the train.

The man stopped at Kase's seat and cleared his throat. "Tickets". His thick bushy eyebrow raised seeing how young Kase looked. "Bit young to be travelin' this time o' night ain't ya?" His eyes narrowing with suspicion.

"No!" Kase insisted, trying not to sound defensive. "not at all, I need a ticket to the city please" he added.

The guard didn't move, "you don't look a day over twelve, do your parents know where you are?"

Kase was a little insulted by this, he knew he looked young but twelve! "I'm seventeen and my parents are none of your concern". He reached into his pocket for some of the notes he stole.

The guard spluttered a little "I'm sorry, jus' askin', no need to be rude". He reached out a hand to take the money before handing over a ticket, "Here you go lad" he said before quickly scurrying off down the train.

Kase put the ticket away in his pocket and soon started to feel tired, moments later he fell asleep. His usual nightmare had changed. The words making up the bars of his prison were still as rigid as ever. This time however he had his backpack in there with him. He unzipped it and found his newly acquired screwdriver, he slammed it between the bars and yanked it down freeing the bar. He did this with each word. Only then did he crawl out of that cage and happily saunter to the doorway and through it.

It was the first time he had not woken up repeating his usual chant of "CAR", "CANT", "RED", "PAIN". The train not only carried his body to freedom, but he had freed his mind too.

CHAPTER TWO

Steve opened his eyes straining against the brightness of the beaming sun. A chorus of birds chirping created a beautiful harmonious melody. He shivered from the ground chill stealing the heat from his already cold body, all that covered him was a thin blanket. He and Mandy found a beautiful spot to bed down after the events of last night. It was off the beaten track and encircled in trees, filled with falling amber leaves.

There was a short stone wall that offered some protection from the wind, leaves on the floor offered a little padding from the firm wet floor. He turned toward her and watched as she shivered in her sleep. Guilt panged through his mind, she deserved better than this. He stood up and covered her with his thin and tattered blanket, trying to shield her from the harsh winter day. He started to move between the trees and relieved himself, whilst taking in his surroundings. He noticed a hawthorn bush in the distance and decided to gather up some breakfast.

He walked on over and picked some of the berries, growing at the foot of the trees he saw some mushrooms sprouting up between the roots. He examined the gills and the cap of the mushroom, Poplar Fieldcap he identified triumphantly, picking some to bring back to Mandy. He set down his supplies and pulled out a little gas cooker and pan from his backpack. He poured in a little water from a bottle and tore up the mushrooms, helping himself to a few berries as he works.

The mushroom broth bubbled away nicely as his eyes settled back on Mandy, her face had taken on a peaceful expression and her shivering had calmed. The birds still chirped their song high above, living rough in the forest had its up points as much as it had its downfalls. Soon they would be back in the city and forced back to the hustle and bustle of life on the bottom rung of society.

His nostrils were being invaded by the strong earthy scent of the pan next to him, bringing him back from his pondering to his current reality. The broth was done, it was time to wake her. He stroked her hair, brushing a stray tuft from her face. She smiled in her sleep. His hand dropped to her shoulder and he gently shook her. "Mandy, Mandy", he spoke softly to her rousing her from slumber. She sat up, still clutching her blankets and kissed him softy. "Morning, lover",

"Morning, I have some breakfast for you, I hope you slept well".

"Better than last night", she scoffed. He tilted his head disapprovingly and held out a hand of the berries. "We also have mushroom broth",

"Well hopefully these ones don't send me to hospital!"

"NO! They are Fieldcap's, they are *definitely* safe. Anyway, we need all the energy we can get, we have a long journey today". Mandy had a mouthful of berries and could only muster a surprised hum. She swallowed the bitter berries, observing him carefully, "Where we going?"

"Like I said last night, to the city. You deserve a better life than this, there will be work there, and I can look after you better. We should be able to hitchhike most of the way, but we will still have quite the walk".

"OH! You were serious, last time we were in the city it didn't work out, we got robbed, attacked, I nearly got raped! We can't stay on the streets; we would need a shelter".

"I know, but I'm going do everything I can to get a better life for you, we can work out the details when we arrive".

"Do we have any money?" she asked as she reached into her own jeans. Steve also took to his feet and mirrored her. He pulled out a number of coins and fingered them as he counted. "sixteen thirty-four". He announces grimacing. She looked down and exhaled with irritation, "I have twenty-two ninety".

"Well, we started out with nothing", he tried to reassure her.

"Yeah, and we still got most of it". She quipped back playfully.

"I think we should get going, try and get as far as we can in the daylight". With that they had finished the Broth and berries, packed away the small camping stove and blankets.

They both looked around at the serene clearing that was their home for the night, they gave it a little wave, then started their slow march towards the road in the distance.

***

It had taken a few hours to arrive at the road. It was deserted, hopes of hitchhiking dissipated quickly. They decided to rest for a moment and take stock. "What direction do we head?" Mandy asked as she slumped down and sat in the overgrown grass.

Steve just shrugged and turned back to the road.

They both sat for a moment before Steve pointed

left. Still no traffic. Luckily, the road had quite a large grass verge that allowed them to walk with relative safety. They both walked single file, staying as far away from the road as possible.

Mandy was walking behind him, her eyes fixated on the empty road, "Let's try and get a lift, off one of these cars then Steve", she scoffed.

He thought for a moment and decided it was best to remain silent. They had been walking for twenty minutes more before the angry rush of a motor could be heard in the distance. They both stopped and faced the road. Steve held up his hand as if hailing a taxi just in time for the car to race past them both at a speed that looked well above the limit. Defeated they continued forwards.

The day dragged horrifically, a number of cars had zoomed past them, each time they stopped and attempted to flag the driver down. The sun was getting lower in the sky and hope was failing them both.

Steve kept trying to keep Mandy's spirits up but even he had to admit, this was looking to be a lost cause and a long walk. "Mandy, can you hear that?".

They both stopped walking, ears tilted to the distance, hope washed over him. He was sure this time, this time they would stop. "I think it's a tractor".

Mandy clearly did not share his enthusiasm, her

voice had not lifted nor had her eyes lit like Steve's, "I can't even see it".

"You know I'm right", Steve turned to her, trying to placate her.

All she could offer was a bland "Yeah, probably".

They kept their eyes focused on the bend in the road as the rumble of the motor got louder. The tractor slowly crawled around the corner and into sight. In the distance it looked to be a mix of green and red however as it neared, the red was indeed a heavy coating of rust.

The tractor was extremely weathered, and it was plodding along at a startlingly slow pace. It had a small cab which was covered with a liberal coating of dirt and mud. The tractor approached the couple and Steve waved enthusiastically, again trying to flag the man down.

As it pulled level and continued forward Mandy raised her hands to her cranium. Steve however maintained eye contact with the cab. The tractor was a few meters ahead as it slowly started to veer into the grassy verge and came to an eventual stop on the long road. Steve bursts into a brisk jog to meet the driver who had stuck his head out the cracked window.

"Hello there!" the driver called out with friendly cadence in his voice.

Steve came to a stop next to the vehicle, catching his breath before calling back in his friendliest tone, "Hi".

"What you doing all the way out here, Have you broken down?"

"Oh! No, we were 'camping', we're trying to get into the city".

"Well, it's about sixty miles that way", the driver pointed back the way he had travelled.

"How long have you been walking?" Steve's face dropped momentarily; he was in for it if Mandy found out.

His face quickly regained its composure, "We been walking for a few hours now".

Mandy had just arrived by his side, finally catching up. The driver looked at her and nodded a greeting to her.

"Well, I aint going to the city in this old thing. I live a few miles down the way. If you want, I can give you a lift to me farmhouse, I aint going into city but I can get you as close as the town on the outskirts, it'll only be a few miles from there".

Steve was overjoyed, "Well that's awfully kind of you sir, that sounds great".

Mandy coughed loudly, loud enough to get Steve's attention. "Steve, can I have a word with you!", she spoke quickly then walked a few steps back out of earshot. Steve flushed red a little but excused himself, quickly moving by her side. "We are not fucking going to that man's farm", she whispered quickly.

"Why not, what's the problem?"

"The last time we had a TV, I watched the Texas chainsaw massacre… I'm fairly sure he was in it too".

Steve laughed heartily, "So, he's an actor in a tractor, that's great" he again laughed before grabbing her hand and leading her back to the man. "Thanks. That would be great, really appreciated."

"Well, hop in then." He scooted back to the other side and opened the cab door, leaning over to offer a hand up. Steve accepted this eagerly, offering the same to Mandy. There wasn't much room, but she made do with half perching on his lap. The man started up the old machine with a twist of a key, a roar, a rumble and it began to slowly creep forward on the straight expanse of road before them.

Steve was excited that they finally managed to get a ride, things were working out. He noticed there had been silence for an awkward period of time, "This is right beauty" he said as he tapped the dash, attempting to break the silence.

The man eagerly nodded agreement "She's an old girl now though", he looked over and smiled. Luckily, he didn't notice Mandy roll her eyes.

"You had her from new?"

"Yeah, she's done some graft, she has." Steve nodded knowingly, "I'm sorry, I didn't catch your name".

"Henry, and yours?"

"I'm Steve and this is Mandy, it's a mighty fine thing you're doing for us Henry. We both really appreciate the ride."

"Well to tell you the truth, it's nice to have some company, it's not very often I see other people." Mandy stirred as they hit a little bump in the road which caused them all to bounce off the seat in the cab.

"Oh, so not married then Henry?" she enquired.

"No, I was married for forty years, she passed six months ago. Sadly, the kids don't come and see me anymore, they all have their own families to worry about."

Mandy looked at the floor, "Sorry" she murmured genuinely.

"That's ok, she was a good woman, too good for me! We had forty beautiful years, and she would be mad as hell if I was moping about!"

The rest of the journey passed quickly, Steve and Henry were talking about agriculture and the joys of simple living whilst Mandy joined in with some funny quips about the joys of running water. They all ended up having a rather pleasant journey down the road and barely noticed the forty-minute ride had passed at all.

The tractor approached a sharp right turn down a thin dirt road. Steve looked out the window and still saw no buildings, but he did notice a beautiful orchard on a far glade and a slow-moving stream running next to the road. Shortly a small blur on the horizon started to expand.

A farmhouse grew into view, he was impressed at the size of the building. It was built of amber stone and had a dark slate roof, there was ivy growing up the front and beautiful rolling beds of wildflowers in boxes under the windows. A pond was located at the side of the property and outbuildings to the other. At the front of one of the outbuildings was a caravan, it was in good condition and modern, looking a little out of place alongside the beauty of the rustic home.

Henry stopped short of the house near a Land Rover, securing the vehicle and offering to help the pair down.

Mandy took his hand and jumped down "Blood hell Henry, that's your house is it, it's massive".

Steve jumped down and just stood taking in the rural beauty "Wow!"

Henry looked back at the farmhouse, "Yeah that's it,

home sweet home".

He started walking over to the front door, a sturdy wooden white door made of wooden slats. He beckoned them over and they followed eagerly.

"I think it's time for a cuppa then I'll show you around." They both nodded appreciatively.

He walked up to the door pushing at the handle and it opened without need for a key. They again both turned to each other, nodded then followed suit. Instinctively, Steve held the door to allow Mandy inside first.

Henry was already somewhere in the bright airy house "Do you mind taking your boots off?" he called out amidst clangs of crockery and the chimes of cutlery.

They both complied dutifully, placing them on the unit by the door, next to Henry's. They called out a confirmation and made their way to the source of commotion.

They walked into the most beautiful, if not a little dated, country kitchen. Oak coloured cabinets lined the walls and slate counter tops accentuated the kitchen. A metal kettle was atop an aga, bubbling and starting to steam.

Henry had already lined up three cups, saucers, and spoons. He took the steaming kettle and splashed the water into the three cups. As Henry finished making the teas Steve took in the kitchen, Mandy was busy looking at little figurines on a tall dresser. Steve couldn't help but notice how immaculately clean everything was, there weren't even any dishes in the white porcelain Belfast sink. Henry handed them both a cup and bid them to follow him.

They followed tentatively, not wishing to spill any liquid on the beautiful hardwood floor. They walked into a carpeted living area. This room was large with a dining table and had many shelves filled with trinkets and books.

He continued through the room to another cosy space with three old but well-conditioned sofas. "This is the telly room, if you go through that arch-way, there are some stairs which will take you to a downstairs bathroom."

He placed his drink down on the small side table and proceeded to sit, exhaling a sigh of relief. He motioned for them to take a seat, and they gladly followed.

"Henry, you have a really nice home". Steve held up a distanced 'cheers' to him before taking a sip of his drink.

"Yes, it's lovely" Mandy proudly added.

They stopped and chatted for a little whilst drinking their tea's. They discussed the farm, his wife, and the house. Steve and Mandy both took care to offer vague responses to Henry's questions, not wanting to disclose too much to a relative stranger, albeit a kind one.

After a natural break in the conversation and a short silence, "So what do you want for dinner?" Henry asked, making great effort to stand.

The pair looked at each other, not really knowing how to answer. "Anything you have, well, we would be very thankful for anything."

Steve nodded, re-affirming Mandy's response. Henry looked at them both with a little concern, "I'll tell you what, why don't you go upstairs and have a bath, I'll make us all something to eat."

Steve started to protest, "We can't put you out like that, you've already been too kind". Mandy's face scrunched slightly, clearly displeased about the idea of a bath being dangled in front of her, then taken away.

Henry noticed this and shook his head, "Nonsense!".

Steve went to interject, but Henry held up his hand to stop any interruption. "Now, both of you listen here. You are my guests, I offered to take you into town, if I'm honest I am nackered. It's been a long day! So, I would rather drive you tomorrow, there is a caravan out front, you are welcome to stay there tonight. As my guests, I'm going to cook some dinner up and if I can say it delicately, after your hike, you are not *washed up* for dinner." Henry's face flashed a little red, and his eyes moved to the floor. "It really would be nice to have some company for a night too, it has been a lonely time since she passed."

Steve saw a glint of shame in Mandy's face, He felt it in himself too. They were indeed filthy in this kind man's beautiful home.

Steve just looked down and softly uttered a low "Thank you".

Henry's face changed back to a smile, "Well that settles it! Now let me show you to the bathroom upstairs."

He led them back out into the hallway and upstairs "Watch out for the beams" he called back, ducking.

He showed them the bathroom which was a stunning flagstone tiled floor with a large ivory roll-topped bath. There were some bottles of bath-salts and other lotions and potions, "I never did dispose of her bits, help yourself to anything." There was a free-standing shower in the corner of the room next to the toilet basin.

"Towels!" Henry exclaimed loudly.

He led them into a bedroom directly opposite the bathroom. It was a somewhat basic room, compared with the rest of the nick-nack covered house. It had large wardrobes of oak and a large double bed, but not much else. He walked over to the door closest to the window and retrieved two giant white bath sheets and plonked them on the bed. I take it you haven't got a change of clothes with you, judging by the size of your backpack. Steve shook his head, again shame wriggled in his belly.

"Right!" Henry bobbed his head decisively, "Everything in the wardrobes here are old clothes that I've been meaning to donate to charity, some of mine, my wife's, and my son's. Help yourself to everything you need."

Henry went to leave but pre-empting any objections he continued "Bring your clothes down to be washed, and I don't want to hear any more about it. Take your time and come down when you're ready" with that, he disappeared back downstairs before any more words could be exchanged.

Steve and Mandy were in a stunned silence, their eyes met and after a few moments of realisation their faces lit up. They quickly disappeared into the bathroom, towels in hand. "Look at the size of the bath Steve, we could both fit in that."

"No, we will!" he smiled with boyish excitement, "We should have a shower first though" he added.

Mandy nodded and started fiddling with the taps and then turned her attention to the shelf of bath oils, carefully selecting and sniffing them before liberally adding them to the tub. While she did this Steve stripped off, peeling back the layers of filthy garments until he was totally naked.

He stepped behind her silently and slapped her bum as she was bent over, causing a giggle to escape her lips. She also stripped down naked, seeing this, Steve whistled causing her to blush.

"Stop it you" she said with mock outrage.

He held the shower door open for her, "M' lady" he said as he bowed.

In the shower she scrubbed herself thoroughly using more soap than she had seen in the last year. Steve just stood and watched her, enjoying the view he proudly displayed his erection for her. She was done quickly, emerging from the cubicle like a new person.

She saw his excitement and laughed, "don't take this the wrong way but that doesn't interest me as much as that does," pointing at the bath.

"Fair point", he chuckled, entering the cubicle himself.

The water washed over him, taking the dirt, the shame, the dark memories with it. He soaped himself up enthusiastically, spending maybe a little too much time washing his groin. Shortly after he shut off the shower he sank into the hot beautiful water of the tub with Mandy.

Steve and Mandy were both in the bath and looked relaxed beyond belief. "I can't remember the last time I had a hot bath" Mandy mused aloud. "486 days ago."

"What?"

"That's the last time I had a hot bath".

"You remember that do you?"

"Yeah, it was at that squat, don't you recall" Mandy just shook her head with a rather blank expression. "Yeah, it was when we were up north, near that dump".

"Oh yeah! Is that the last time we had hot water?"

"Yeah!" He nodded. "Then we best make the most of it", she smiled and flicked some water at him. He returned the favour, back and forth before he leaned in and passionately kissed her, "I do love you Mandy".

"I love you back".

"Come on then, we should get out".

"Well, you first, I'll come join you in a minute or two", Steve just nodded and proceeded to stand up, stepped over to the bathmat and dried himself off. He wrapped the towel around himself, applied deodorant from the shelf and left Mandy to herself in the tub, closing the door behind him. He entered the bedroom and opened the wardrobe.

He scanned the hangers for a little while, there is so much to choose from, he wondered to himself, did Henry really intend to donate **all** of this to charity? He pulled out a blue and white checked shirt with thin pink threads running through it. It felt really high quality. As he removed the shirt, he spotted a light, stonewashed pair of jeans. Again, the jeans felt like high-quality soft denim. He dropped the towel and pulled the jeans off the hanger.

Steve hesitated; he didn't want to have to 'go commando' but his pants were beyond salvation. He rummaged in the drawers and found a sealed pack of ladies' pants, "maybe not" he chuckled, throwing them on the bed. After a little more rummaging, he found some boxers, a white t shirt, and a few pairs of balled up socks. He pulled them on and heaved the rest of the clothes on too.

The door opened and Mandy entered the room wrapped in a towel. She wolf-whistled at him, causing him to turn towards her and scowl. Behind her was a full-length mirror hidden by the door, he caught a glimpse of himself, he was gobsmacked, he felt amazing. This was a feeling that had escaped him for years, he felt like a part of society again. Mandy had a serene smile, "You look like the man I married again, handsome". She walked to the wardrobe herself and flicked through some of the garments. "Where did he get women's clothes from? Do you think they are his wife's?"

"Where else would he have got them from?" he answered laughing, still unable to take his eyes from the mirror.

"I'm not wearing a dead woman's clothes Steve".

"Well, you don't want to put your other ones back on, do you?"

"Well, no, but..." Steve cut across her, "But nothing my love, just put them on, then get downstairs. I found a new pack of panties in the cupboard. I threw them on the bed. I'm going to clean the bathroom up, make sure it's all clean and dry."

Mandy nodded and looked back towards the wardrobe unconvinced. Steve grabbed his towel and walked out of the room, back to the bathroom. He used his towel to dry the bathtub making sure there was no oily residue left. He also dried the floor before going to the shower. It had big dirt streaks on the walls which he rinsed off with the shower head before drying it. He looked around at his handywork. Satisfied, he gathered up both of their clothes in the towel and took them with him downstairs.

As he walked down the staircase his nose was alerted to a beautiful aroma. Pastry and gravy enticed him into the kitchen where Henry stood mashing potatoes. Henry turned to acknowledge Steve, "Well you look a lot better, it's good to see the threads fit you well".

"Yeah, thank you Henry, I feel human again, I can't say it enough, thank you." Henry pointed to the utility room adjacent to the kitchen and motioned him to put the laundry inside.

"It's nothing, I can't even get into them these days, at least they're not going to go to waste."

Steve felt moved but remained silent, allowing Henry to continue with his preparations. Mandy could be heard walking down the stairs before she entered the kitchen, "Wow! The food smells amazing Henry!", she exclaimed.

"Thank you and you look better as well my darling" Henry declared magnanimously.

Mandy blushed slightly "Thanks, for the clothes, for everything".

Henry didn't turn back to continue cooking, he just stared, "You know, it's nice to see that outfit again, my wife wore it the day she passed".

Mandy turned very pale, not quite sure how to respond. Steve's eyes darted between him and Mandy. Nobody made a sound for a tense couple of seconds, this felt like the longest silence before Henry burst out laughing.

The pair both looked uncomfortable, but Henry continued, "I'm joking, I'm sorry it was in bad taste. I think my daughter in law left that here last time she was here. I have a bit of a dark humour sometimes. I apologise."

Mandy remained silent for a second, exhaling a sigh of relief before laughing, "Jesus, you had me going".

Steve however was laughing hysterically. Henry turned back to the cooker where peas were simmering away nicely, "Right do you want a drink?".

They both eagerly accepted the offer. Henry put them both to work setting the table, pointing at an array of cabinets and drawers where things were neatly stored. Before long, the table in the dining room was fit for a feast, cutlery, crockery and condiments were all neatly laid out, as were three wine glasses and three icy bottles of beer. Henry instructed them to have a seat, handing them a bowl to carry with them.

Shortly they were all seated at the large dining table which could have easily accommodated three times as many people. The table was suitably filled with peas, carrots, potatoes, gravy, and a rather large pie. The aroma of the beautifully home cooked food reminded them how hungry they really were.

Henry was already helping himself to the vegetable when he noticed the pair sat there, "Dig in" he prompted, handing Mandy the bowl of peas he had in his hand.

With that, they did while Henry poured the wine for them all.

Steve was having a liberal second helping of the pie, which in his very learned opinion, was the single most beautiful thing he had ever tasted. Mandy had already had her fill and was sipping her drink. Through the meal, they all chatted pleasantries, but a contented silence had overtaken the table.

Bottle of wine empty, Henry took a swig of his beer, "So what do you two do?".

Mandy looked at Steve, he glanced over at her before responding "Well, we are both sort of between jobs at the moment".

"Oh, that's right, you said you wanted to get to the city".

Mandy chimed in, "Yeah we'll find some work, get back on our feet".

Henry nodded pleasantly, "Where you planning on staying? Are you staying with some friends until you get everything straight?".

A thought crossed Steve's mind; did he know that they were homeless? Did he just think of them as lost ramblers? Would he be as hospitable if he knew? He was a fairly good judge of character, and Henry seemed like a good man, but he didn't want to test their luck.

The pair both flashed a nervous grimace, "We aren't too sure whom we are staying with yet, probably some friends" Steve offered up loosely.

Henry nodded somewhat unconvinced, "Well, where did you stay last night? You said you camped but I didn't see a tent or anything. When I got to you, you were in the middle of nowhere".

Mandy shifted nervously in her seat before she blurted out, "Yes, we camped, our tent blew away".

"Bloody hell, I bet it was cold last night", Henry replied sounding a little more convinced, although Steve was not so sure as he quickly dropped the subject.

Everyone had finished eating, "Was that meal alright for everyone?".

The pair enthusiastically bobbed their heads, "I'm stuffed mate, thanks" Steve called out.

"It was lovely, really we can't thank you for all that you have done", Mandy added.

Henry stood up and started to gather the plates up, Mandy outstretched her hand and rested it on Henry's, "Sod off Henry, there is no way you're clearing up as well, I'll do it. Why don't you both go and chill out in the other room!"

Henry smiled, "Do you want to Steve?".

Steve smiled contentedly, "It's your house, it's up to you".

"Come on then, bring some more beers in."

Henry ambled into the other room, leaving Steve

and Mandy alone for a moment. He kissed her on the cheek and left to fetch some more beers. On the way back he handed one to Mandy and took the others to Henry in the TV room.

CHAPTER THREE

Mandy started to clear everything from the table, even though Henry had put out quite the spread, barley scraps remained now. She ran a sink of hot soapy water to carefully wash all the pots and pans, paying extra care to the crockery.

Washing up all completed, she returned to wipe down the table. She decided to check with the lads to see if they needed any more drinks, they were fine. She tenderly dried all the soapy utensils, taking care to find the proper location for each item before storing it away. She stood and double checked her work, ensuring she didn't miss anything. Cleaning completed, all that was left to do was to join the men in the lounge.

As she walked into the room carrying her beer the two men were seated on comfy armchairs next to each other, laughing heartily. She plonked herself down on a nearby sofa and took a deep sip of her beer.

Henry motioned to her, "You alright, my dear?"

She nodded, "Actually could I just use your bathroom?"

He motioned to the archway at the far end of the room, "Yes of course, just follow the hallway along". He also stood up; "I'm going to get us all another round of beers from the fridge".

He returned with two frothy bottles of beer, a bottle of whiskey, and a little bucket of ice. He handed Steve a bottle and left one on the side table next to Mandy's empty bottle.

"I'm double parked here Henry" Steve laughed.

Henry just chuckled as he grabbed a glass from the cabinet in the corner and plonked himself back in his chair.

Mandy returned to her chair and thanked Henry for the drink. "So, have you lived here long?"

"I was born here, farms been in the family years, it has." They both raised an eyebrow, Steve started to think about his own childhood, they moved around a lot with his father performing all over the country. He never really had that level of stability.

"Can I ask you a question?", Steve asked.

Henry nodded graciously so Steve pressed on. "Why have you done this for us, I mean you have not only given us a ride, but let us clean up, given us clothes, fed us, watered us, and now your providing drinks! Why would you do that? I mean you don't know us from Adam, do you?"

Henry looked for a moment as if he were offended, did he need a reason to be kind? His warm smile returned before he spoke. "If I'm honest, I don't get to see a lot of people these days. Most of my friends and family are dead, my kids don't want to know me. I really am enjoying having some company. On a more serious note, I feel if I'd drove straight past you today and I read something had happened, I don't think I could of ever forgive myself. I saw on the news just last week that a body was found not too far away from here on the moors. It feels like there is always something bad happening."

Steve was so moved by his statement he stood up and walked over to him, hand outstretched to him to shake. Henry stood up took his hand, shaking it enthusiastically. He walked over and retrieved another glass from the cabinet. "Leave that beer, Mandy seems to be enjoying them and it's the last one, have a whiskey with me".

Steve happily accepted, he took the beer and went to hand it to Mandy, she was fast asleep, clutching her empty beer bottle. Steve took it from her and placed them both on the side table next to her. "A decent meal must have zonked her out!" he thought.

Steve took a seat next to Henry, nursing his whiskey. "Henry, can I be honest with you."

He just continued to sip his drink, waiting for Steve to proceed.

"Me and Mandy we weren't camping last night, our tent didn't fly away; we have been homeless for the last few years. I'm sorry we weren't honest with you but we both worried that we would make you suspicious of us, worried we would try and take something."

Henry did not look shocked at all, he just nodded in acknowledgement.

"We were in a squat house last night, part of a row of houses to be demolished on a new development. Security came and chased us out in the middle of the night. That's why we slept outside in the freezing cold."

Henry considered for a moment before he spoke, "I understand".

His face however looked confused, maybe he could not fathom the idea of not knowing where you would be sleeping, or how to cope without stability and safety of having a home, Steve mused to himself.

There was a sprawling silence before Henry spoke again. "If I may ask, and feel free not to answer, how did you become Homeless?"

Steve looked over at Mandy who was still unconscious. He didn't like talking about their past but Henry deserved to know, especially after all of his kindness. His eyes focused on a specific point in the carpet pattern and he spoke softly.

"Me and Mandy have been together since she left school, she liked that it was *naughty* that I was a little older. It had not always been plain sailing, but we always made it through. We always had each other's back. We got married when she was in her mid-twenties, we bought a house and we tried to start a family. We tried but couldn't conceive so we took it as a sign that it wasn't meant to be.

"We tried to live well and be happy, but Mandy lost her job in the recession. She secretly started gambling as a way to cope. It was bingo at first, then fruit machines then horses. I didn't realise how bad the problem was until I was also made redundant. I thought we could make it through, tighten our belts, benefits were a pittance, at least it was something coming in. We fell behind on the mortgage then one day our credit card was declined in the supermarket."

Steve took a long sip of his drink and Henry instinctively topped up his glass. Henry had a face twisted with equal shock and intrigue.

"It was weird, we had long paid off that card, I thought because of inactivity it had been blocked. I mean we only increased the limit to buy a new car years before. There should have been over 10 thousand available. It should have been empty! When I called the bank, it was maxed out, savings empty. I went home and confronted Mandy, she confessed everything; her depression her misery not being able to have a family."

Henry's eyes fell to the floor as Steve continued.

"It turned out she had been pregnant a number of times, but within the first few weeks of the pregnancy, she would miscarry. She felt responsible and couldn't bear to tell me, she worried I would blame her too. It broke her, Henry".

Steve paused again and looked towards Mandy who still hadn't awoken, her angelic face showing no signs of the sadness she had endured. Henry looked towards Mandy and then back to the Steve and his stoic expression.

"She had told me she had stopped gambling, but she hadn't. It all came to a head when she missed her sign on at the Jobcentre. Apparently, she could not stop feeding the machine. It was a joint claim, so the sanctions applied to the both of us. I found her out of her mind, mid overdose. When she got out of the hospital, we had lost the house. We lived in the car for a while. I still loved her and asked her why she did it. Her response haunted me; it still does to this day. She thought with all the bad luck, the loss, the universe owed her something, when she lost all our money, she thought the best gift she could give me, would be her death.

"That was a turning point, that's when she promised me the gambling was over with. If she didn't have the strength, she could have all of mine. Even living in our car, we tried to find rental housing, our credit was bad, so we sold the car to get a deposit together for a bedsit. The landlord was a scammer and took our money.

"We were left with nothing. She pawned her engagement ring and wedding band behind my back, just so we had money to eat. Don't laugh, but

I made her a new one out of things we found on the beach. I loved her more than any money, more than any house, more than my own life, she is my queen, my soulmate. My world. She blames herself, but it was not her fault. She couldn't help the emptiness of losing our babies, she couldn't help the economy or the lack of support."

Steve finished speaking, his entire history exposed. He felt a little ashamed of his past, but he knew he owed Henry at least that. Henry sat looking at him and spoke softly, "I'm sorry for everything that happened to you". Steve bowed his head, profoundly moved by the lack of judgement. "If I'm honest, I knew she was not well for a long time, I was too scared to address it. We fell together and we will rebuild the same way. Together." Steve finished.

Henry really did not know what to say, he appreciated his candour. Their appearance made more sense after hearing their tale. He knew he had to do what he could to help them, after all he knew that intense feeling of loyalty before his wife passed. He felt the same way about her when she was alive. He would have happily given everything he had, everything he owned for another day with his beloved.

"I respect what you have done, I respect that you have stayed together, If I was in your position, I would have given everything for my wife too" he proudly reassured.

Steve felt warmth in his heart, he clinked glasses with Henry and they both drank from their glasses. The sound must have woken Mandy as she sat up straight and stretched.

"Sorry Henry, I must have drifted off after that beautiful meal. I wasn't out too long, was I?" she enquired politely.

Henry laughed, "Only about half an hour".

Steve pointed at the little table near the side of the sofa, I put you another beer on the side if you want it.

"Oh! and you're on the hard stuff, are you?" she said with mock indignance.

Henry again chuckled and stood to get another glass from the cabinet, placing it on the table by Mandy.

Steve's eyes followed Henry, next to the cabinet was a fabric bag that looked like a guitar case. His eyes lit up, "Henry, do you play" he asked pointing at the black fabric case.

Henry looked around and spotted what he was pointing to. "Yeah, I did a little, many years ago. My hands are shot now, I can barely tie a shoe" Henry laughed bitterly.

Steve smiled sympathetically, "Would you mind?" he said pointing to himself.

Henry walked over fetching it back to his chair. He unzipped the case and took out a beautiful acoustic guitar. It had oak details and a deep mahogany fret leading to the black and red body. Henry took a duster from the side of his chair and lovingly polished the framework before handing it over.

"Here you are."

Steve gently plucked the strings and fiddled with

the tuning pegs; ear tilted down towards the instrument. He rested the body on his knee and started playing a little riff, which developed into a melody. Henry's eyes widened, and his head started bopping in time. Mandy perked up too, it had been a long time since she heard him play. Steve finished playing, placing the plectrum back in between the strings at the top.

Steve placed the guitar back in the bag "Yeah not a bad sound out of that, is there?"

Henry face was agog, "You play very well".

"Thank you, I used to make them before we lost everything. I've made a few on the streets too."

Henry was quite taken aback, "Out of what?" he asked incredulously.

"Any old tat really, dust bin lids and broom handles, scrap metal, driftwood, anything really. They will have all been smash to bits now, we left the last place in a rush" he said wistfully.

Steve stood up and placed it back in the corner by the cabinet. While he was stood up, he looked at Henry, "Not to be rude but do you mind if I went to sleep now. The day is catching up with me" He asked politely.

Mandy also yawned after downing the last of her drink.

Henry smiled genuinely, "No, not at all. You know

where the spare bedroom is".

Mandy went to stand but paused, "Oh, I thought we were staying in the caravan".

Henry laughed and reassured them "No go upstairs, I think you kids have had more than your fair share of rough nights. Feel free to have the spare room".

Mandy nodded as she got to her feet, "If you're sure, we would appreciate it".

Mandy led the way out the room, and Steve followed her. They both called back their thanks and appreciation back to Henry who just waved off their thanks as unnecessary. The final call of "goodnight" and they were gone.

CHAPTER FOUR

It was dark and still outside, even the heavy draperies on the window were not subjected to the movement of the wind. The pair were in the bed asleep when a noise suddenly erupted outside. Mandy did not stir; she was in a wonderful dreamland of luxury. Afterall, it had been many years since she felt the comfort and safety of a luxurious bed. Steve, however, was used to being on high alert, always ready to protect Mandy from any nefarious event. He recognised the sound as water. He listened for a moment, water, silence, movement, creaking. Silence was again washed over the room. His eyes darted around the room; he momentarily had forgotten where he was.

The events of the previous day came tumbling back to him, the farm, the food, Henry. He slipped out of the bed, standing naked and stretching, eyes casting a loving stare over Mandy's sleeping frame. He quietly pulled on his clothes and slipped out of the room, taking every precaution not to wake his sleeping wife. Now free of the room he quietly made his way downstairs, the wood creaking quietly below him. From the bottom of the stairs, he could see Henry leaning against the counter. He walked into the kitchen to greet Henry who was quietly lost in thought, sipping a cup of tea. "Morning!" He greeted him quietly, stirring Henry from his daydream.

He greeted Steve with a friendly smile and walked over to the aga to boil water for his guest. "You're up early", Henry said kindly.

"Well, I heard you getting up, I just thought you might need a hand with something".

Henry chuckled, "Very kind, but there was no need for you to get up".

Steve shook his head, "Nonsense, I want to help out".

"Well, in that case you should have a cuppa before we start, it always sorts me out" Henry turned back to the steaming kettle and poured a tea, handing it over.

"If I knew you were getting up, I would have had one ready".

They both drank in silence, Steve was still trying to come to terms with the morning battling his sleepy brain to wake. The tea did help.

From across the kitchen Steve watched Henry put the cup in the sink, "Right you ready?" he asked.

Steve followed suit and nodded. They both left the kitchen and went to the front door. They quickly put on their boots and left into the dark hue of the morning.

***

A beam of sunlight shone on Mandy's face, it roused her from a sweet, gentle slumber. She opened her eyes to take in her surroundings, she felt refreshed and wholly invigorated. She sat up in bed to get the sunlight from her face. The heavy drapes were blocking out all the light bar a little crack where they met. As she was sitting there, she mused about the events of the previous day. Suddenly her mind went to Steve, she turned her head, he wasn't in bed with her.

She pulled back the duvet and stepped onto the carpet, gathering up clothes and dressing swiftly. She walked into the hallway and downstairs to the kitchen. Two cups sat in the sink, she called out for Steve and Henry, but silence was her only reply. She wondered around, a little curious until she noticed that two pairs of boots were missing from the rug at the front door. "they must have gone out" she mused to herself. She went back to the kitchen and made herself a tea and drank it whilst standing inspecting the view from the kitchen window, looking out at the rolling farmlands surrounding the house.

There was nothing else for it, she would go back to the bedroom and make the bed, then have a shower. Nodding her head, she placed the empty cup in the sink and left the room. In the bedroom she started by drawing back the curtains, warm soothing light flooded the room, her eyes taking a moment to adjust. She plumped the pillows and pulled the sheet and duvet before getting a towel and walking into the bathroom.

She helped herself to some more lotions and potions making sure to spend extra time washing her hair. She dried quickly and re-dresses cleaning the bathroom down as she did. She took extra time taking in the beauty of the home she had been welcomed into, there was an urge to explore the rest of the rooms, but she didn't want to invade Henry's privacy. Mandy noticed a knot in the back of her hair.

She took a pair of scissors from the cabinet and gave herself a little trim, she felt like a new woman. She arrived back at the kitchen, clean and dry. She recalled the utility room at the back, so she took her towel and placed it in the hamper. Her old clothes were clean and dry in another machine. She unloaded it and folded all the contents. Behind her was a vacuum cleaner, she took it and hoovered up all the hair from the floor in the bathroom, she continued to do the same for the bedroom they spent the night in.

Downstairs she collected all the glasses and empty bottles from the living room and cleared them all into the kitchen. She ran some water and washed up the bits she had found. While she had it, she decided to run the hoover round the downstairs too.

The house was immaculate again, she was proud of her work. It had been too long since she could take the pleasure of a clean house, even if it wasn't hers. A rumble of hunger emanated from her stomach, "it wouldn't hurt to look" she thought. The fridge was full of food, she considered for a moment and decided she was going to cook a full English breakfast for them all, as a thank you to their gracious host.

She grabbed a pan from the rack and placed it on the aga. A low rumble, far in the distance stole her attention for a moment, looking out the window she could see nothing, but the sound surely marked the return of the men. She hurriedly prepared the food and refilled the kettle ready for their arrival. As the food sizzled, releasing an overwhelming breakfast aroma, she set the table taking care with the crockery.

The low rumble turned into a meek roar, she

glanced out the window and this time she spotted the rusty green tractor in in the near distance. She continued to cook up a storm, taking care not to burn any of the ingredients.

The noise stopped abruptly outside the farmhouse, Mandy heard the door click open and the two men walked though laughing heartily.

"Something smells nice Steve", Henry said as he fought to remove his boots.

"It does! You must have other guests, Mandy is a terrible cook, it can't be her!" Steve joked pointedly.

He already had his boots off and was making his way over to his wife to kiss her. Mandy just exhaled loudly before calling out, "It wasn't funny before and it's not funny now Steve!".

She caught his eye and winked, "I've got the kettle on and the food will be ready in a few moments, the tables set so have a seat.

Henry and Steve walked into the dining room, as the pair sat down, they both groaned loudly with the strain of the morning's work. They had barely hit the seats when Mandy walked in, confidently placing a steaming hot drink on the table in front of them both.

She stopped by Henry as she placed his drink down, "Can I get you anything else?"

Steve put his hand up as if he were in a classroom, "I'll have a new back if your taking orders?"

Concern flashed across her face, "You haven't done your back in again have you?"

Steve shook his head vigorously as his hand rubbed his lower spine, "No just a bit sore".

Mandy nodded somewhat sternly and walked back to the kitchen.

Merely a few moments later Mandy walked into the dining room with plates filled with a beautifully cooked breakfast. There was quite the selection, bacon, sausage, egg, mushrooms, potato, beans and some buttered fresh bread.

Mandy placed the plates down and a pang of guilt came over her, "Henry, I hope it's ok I did us all a breakfast. I just realised how much food I've cooked" she looked sheepishly at him.

Henry laughed and waved away her concerns, "Not at all, you didn't have to go to all that effort, but you are welcome to, it is certainly appreciated".

With that they all dug into the hearty meal.

The plates were scraped clean, the three people sat stroking their full stomachs silently, enjoying the full sensation.

Henry eventually broke the silence, "So when do you two need to be off?"

Steve pondered, sitting up at the table, "How far is it to that town you told us about?"

"it's about ten miles, shouldn't take too long."

"Well, we can go whenever you are ready Henry." Steve said, locking eyes with Mandy.

They were both excited for the next part of the journey. It felt like a new beginning. Mandy stood up, placing her hand on the empty plates and started clearing the table down. Henry stood up and told her to leave it for him, but she was adamant. Henry just laughed and took his seat again as Mandy worked.

He turned to Steve "Why don't you grab a few more items from the wardrobe for your journey, your other clothes should be ready now too".

Steve wanted to object, but Henry excused himself and disappeared into the depths of the house. Steve took the opportunity to go back to the room, which was immaculate. He decided to have a shower first after his hard day's work before looking through the wardrobe as instructed.

Out of the shower, he dried himself off then grabbed another pair of jeans, t shirt and a dress shirt, which he thought would be good for an interview. Mandy walked into the room carrying their old clothes. They decided to pack them just in case. The backpack was bulging now with the new clothes they had both selected, they embraced each other and kissed lightly.

He swept her hair off her ear and whispered, "Your hair looks beautiful. You know everything happens for a reason; this is our new start baby!"

She smiled as tears welled in her eyes, she was riding such a high that she didn't just believe him, she knew it to be true.

Their embrace was cut short by a voice from downstairs, "Are you both ready?".

Henry's voice rang through the house, they called back to him and made their way downstairs with their new possessions. Henry smiled at the sight of them, they looked anew, refreshed from when he first met them just the other day. Steve took a deep breath and exhaled slowly before speaking softly,

"We are ready".

***

It was a short enough ride to the little hamlet in the Land Rover, the roads were extremely rural. It struck Steve that not only were they walking in the wrong direction, but they would have been walking for maybe a couple of days before even finding out. There was nothing out here, Henry was a true blessing.

The car pulled up on the main road, just outside

a beautiful Pub. It had some small picnic tables outside and a thatched roof, the building itself was painted white and was accentuated with black painted beams. It was a large building and seemed to go back quite a way. They all got out of the vehicle, Henry was quite sad to see them go, but he was pleased he could help them.

Steve spoke first, "Henry, we can't honestly thank you enough."

He took hold of Henry's hand and shook it wholeheartedly; he was getting a little emotional and couldn't really speak. Mandy just flung herself around him in the warmest of embraces.

All she could manage was a tear filled "Thank you".

The pair went to walk away but Henry stopped them, "Hold up!" he called.

They both turned back to him a little shocked. "My friend Jill runs the pub here; she owed me a favour and has arranged a night's stay here for you. I just told her I had some friends in town so don't worry, I haven't been discussing your business", he winked at Steve as he spoke.

Steve understood this and appreciated it, confessing his past to Henry felt like a release, felt like letting go, but he still didn't want people to know more than they needed to.

The pair stuttered at the revelation of a hotel room,

but Henry continued unperturbed. "This is also yours". He held out an envelope to Steve which he instinctively refused to take.

This was a line he wouldn't cross; he knew there was money in it, he didn't want charity from him. Henry chuckled and took a step towards him, "here", he repeated a little more forcefully. Taking Steve's hand and forcing the envelope into it. "Henry, we don't need your charity, you have already done more than anyone else reasonably would have!", Steve started tentatively.

Henry just laughed, "Charity! These are your wages".

Steve looked at him perplexed so he continued, "from today! For helping out!"

Steve didn't know what to say, how to act, he just stood there agog, envelope in hand. Mandy was looking form one to the other, she was equally moved by the gesture.

Henry turned to leave and the pair both stuttered, he turned back to them again, "Ah and I nearly forgot". He opened the boot of the Land Rover and retrieved a large fabric case, he held it out for Steve to take.

"I can't take that!" Steve said, even though he couldn't take his eyes off it.

Henry again took Steve's hand and gently guided

it to the carry handle. Steve did not resist him. As soon as he had the guitar case in his hand, he wrapped his arms around Henry and gave him a hug, "you have given us so many gifts, the biggest of all is our dignity".

Henry patted Steve's back as they released each other. Mandy ran over and embraced him again too. As soon as he was free, he wiped his eye that had somehow become quite damp, waved, and jumped back in his Land Rover, driving off, out into the distance.

CHAPTER FIVE

Mandy and Steve just stood, looking at each other in a stunned silence for a few moments. They jolted to their senses and decided to make their way inside. They only stopped when a loud honking came from the road behind. It was Henry's Land Rover, he had turned round and slowed down to a sluggish roll. The window open he shouted out, "Hey, I forgot to say, the bus only comes twice a day, so don't miss it!" he waved again and finally drove off waving, not waiting for a reply. They both laughed with each other and walked to the door of the bar.

The inside of the bar was decorated very much in keeping with the age of the building. There was a roaring open fire burning at the far end of the building and a variety of beautiful pictures and painting adorning the walls. Opposite the bar in the corner was a little raised stage with a tattered piano standing firm atop it.

Behind the bar was a pretty, young woman, she could have been no older than her mid-twenties, her long brunette hair was tied back in a pony-tail leaving no obstruction to her features. She had beautiful grey eyes but, her most inviting and prominent feature was her smile. Warm, welcoming, like a smile you would use to greet an old friend.

"Hi, I'm..." Steve began but the woman looked up and spoke over him in a bubbly, welcoming tone.

"Ah! you must be Henry's friends, I'm Jill, I own the pub; I haven't made your room up yet, but I can go and do it now if you want to get up there". She smiled and looked over to Mandy, giving her a little respectful nod. Steve glanced at Mandy before turning back to the woman behind the counter.

"Well, there's no rush we can have a sit down for a bit if you want."

"OK, why don't you make yourselves at home, I'll go and get it sorted for you." With that she left the bar and retired upstairs.

Steve and Mandy selected the regal green armchairs by the fireplace and put the guitar case and backpack down. They both continued to look around before taking their seats. "Nice in here isn't it?" Mandy muttered.

Steve's eyes fixed on the wooden beams running across the ceiling, "Yes, the building is stunning, the fire is beautiful, it's chucking out some heat too". He put his hand out to feel it while Mandy continued quietly, "Do you remember when we last had an open fire?"

"No when was that?" Steve said, an inquisitive look on his face.

"When we were in the West Country." Mandy chuckled a little. "You thought it would be clever to light a fire in the middle of that old, abandoned house we were staying in. You nearly killed yourself" she finished rather more seriously.

Steve's face flashed a little red, but he didn't lose his composure, "I can't recall that one".

"Yes! The fireman pulled you out, and they tried doing you for arson".

Steve's eyes glazed as he stared into space, a mock look of contemplation affixed on his visage, "hmm, maybe I choose to remember it all a little differently".

Mandy's face dropped, she looked annoyed by his stubbornness, but the mock chilly look soon dissipated and was replaced by her usual warmth. Mandy was chuckling when a little voice called over from behind the bar, "There's someone making up the room now, it won't be long".

The woman disappeared back into the heart of the building, leaving the bar again unattended. Steve suddenly stood up from the seat, digging his hand into his pocket to retrieve a scrunched-up envelope.

Mandy perked up, "Ah, I forgot, how much money did Henry give you?"

"us!" he quickly corrected her with a smile.

He poked his finger into the top and tore the envelope open. He pulled out a stack of notes and counted them slowly, "there is two hundred quid here!" Both of them looked at each other with shocked expressions.

There was a stunned silence for a few minutes before Mandy spoke again. "We'll have to pay him back when we get back on our feet."

Steve stared wistfully at the money, "I'll do more than that! I'll get him a new tractor".

Mandy rolled her eyes petulantly, "And when are we going to be able to afford a tractor Steve?" Steve's eyes met hers as he laughed, "Pff, I don't know, but it's the thought that counts, isn't it?" Steve said defensively.

Mandy nodded kindly as she placed her hand on his shoulder, "My thoughtful man".

Changing the subject, he put the money back in his pocket, "Do you think we should have a drink?"

Mandy thought for a moment, "I think we should

just stick to tea for now, we can have a little drink later. I don't want to have too late of a night tonight, we can't miss that bus" she paused for a moment, "what time is the bus anyway?"

"I'll find out" Steve said as he walked towards the bar.

He called out for the Jill, but she didn't materialise. At the end of the bar an older portly man stood up. He was rather tall and had no hair other than a few grey whisps by his ears. He left his stool and walked behind the bar, down towards Steve.

It took a few moments, but he eventually arrived, "What can I do for you boy?" he asked a little force-fully.

"Could I order two teas, also do you know when the bus leaves for the city." Steve replied.

The bloke behind the bar turned to the man he was sitting with and called out, "You know what time the bus leaves?"

The other man lifted his eyes, paused then shook his head. Silently returning his attention to his drink.

"Would Jimmy know?" the man behind the counter called back.

This time his friend spoke up without even looking. He had a strong Scottish accent as he spoke, "You're a silly old sod, Jimmy's been dead five years".

The man in front of Steve shook his head, "Don't know the bus schedule, sorry boy" he said rather gruffly. He didn't wait for another question before he shuffled back to his stool at the end of the bar.

Steve was a little baffled by the conversation, he thought he would try asking Jill when he saw her again. He may get a little more sense from her. He returned to Mandy by the fire and took his seat. "What did he say? She asked hurriedly.

"No, he doesn't, and Jimmy doesn't know either."

"Who's Jimmy, his mate?"

"No Jimmy doesn't know cos he's been dead five years!".

"Oh?"

Mandy's face was awash with confusion upon hearing Steve's words, but she didn't enquire further. A flyer on the mantlepiece had stolen her gaze. She retrieved it, flicking through the pages. It had local information; attractions to visit, local events, and telephone numbers, one thing it didn't have, bus timetables. Steve knew her well enough to read her expression so didn't enquire, he was taking his time looking at the nick-nacks decorating the establishment.

Steve felt an arm on his shoulder, he spun round to see whom it belonged to. Jill stood with her warm, pleasant smile. "Your room is ready." She spoke clearly and respectfully with just the slightest twang of an accent. "Do you need a hand with your bags?" she enquired. The pair just shook their heads and collected their belongings, following her up a stairwell to the right of the bar.

They arrived at a neat little doorway on the second floor. Jill, took a key from her pocket and let the pair in. She followed them inside and showed them where they could find everything. Happy, Jill left the key with Mandy and went to make her exit.

"Oh Jill, we ordered two teas downstairs, we will pop down for them in a moment." Steve mentioned.

"Teas?"

"Yes, I ordered them with the gent downstairs." With that she rolled her eyes, and apologies flooded from her.

"I'm sorry, that's my father, he's a... *few cards short of a deck*." She spoke with a little apprehension, "I'll tell you what, I can bring them up. They are on the house, for keeping you waiting."

Steve and Mandy tried to refuse but she was adamant. She went to leave again but Mandy called out to her, "Jill, one last thing, do you know when the bus to the city leaves? Henry said there's only two a day".

Jills face scrunched up a little, "I'm sorry I don't really know, I'll ask around and try and find out for you". She smiled and within moments she had closed the door and disappeared back into the building.

Steve and Mandy stood staring at the room, it was beautiful, a large double bed lay in the middle of the angled roof eves, a large window stood behind the bed allowing light to bathe the room. A matching dark cherry wood wardrobe stood on the back wall next to the entrance to the en-suite bathroom.

Steve couldn't help but think that it was such a lovely room that Henry must have spent a fortune on it. Steve put his guitar and backpack on the chairs by the entrance door and went to join Mandy in the bathroom. She was admiring the perfectly clean, white, bathtub in the corner. Steve remained quiet, placing his hands on her shoulders, massaging her gently.

A knock at the door distracted them, Jill had returned with the teas, she still didn't know the bus schedule, so with a quick apology she popped the cups down on the table and left them to themselves. They looked at each other, then at the bed, before racing to lay on the bed. They were giggling, "A proper bed two nights in a row, it can't get much better than this".

Steve turned his head to look at her as she spoke. "It's really soft too!" she exclaimed.

He paused for a moment before replying, "You'll

go soft, what happens if we need to sleep rough again?"

His words had a foreboding tone, but she waved the words away, "It will be fine".

Steve continued, "Well I might sleep on the floor".

Mandy laughed, "well then that means I get the whole bed to myself".

Steve raised his eyebrow and exhaled, "You know what, it is soft, maybe I'll give the floor a miss! Anyway, who knows the next time we'll get to sleep in a real bed again?" He turned to look at her and kissed her passionately.

He reached to stroke her breasts, he excitedly undressed and started to make love to her.

***

Mandy rolled over and stepped out of bed and into the bathroom, "Do you think we should eat something later or just save the money?". She called back from the shower.

Steve just lay watching the shadow she was casting on the floor between the rooms. He contemplated her words as he watched the light dancing, remembering the love they had shared in their life together.

Eventually he responded, "See how you feel later

baby, we have eaten well twice in the last two days, I don't want to get used to eating every day."

She stepped out the shower and wrapped herself in a towel, joining Steve on the bed. "Yes, let's see how we feel." Steve kissed her as he stood up, before making his way to the shower.

With the pair dry and dressed they decided to go downstairs to the bar. The daylight had faded from view in the window, without a clock or a watch they had no idea what time it was. They grabbed the empty cups and key as they walked past the small table and walked through the door and down the stairs.

As they arrived on the ground floor of the bar Jill walked past them, she did a doubletake and stopped in front of the pair. "I forgot to mention earlier, Henry asked for me to do you both an evening meal, I can get you a menu." She nodded curtly then walked off without waiting for a reply.

The clock on the wall read quarter to eight. It was getting on in the day, the bar had started to get a little busier. Steve led Mandy over to an empty table, it was in the corner by a coloured glass window.

Steve pulled out a chair for Mandy to sit down, he remained standing. "As the meal is taken care of, Drink?" He asked, smile across his face.

She giggled and nodded enthusiastically, "Vodka honey".

Steve disappeared to the bar and returned with two glasses, filled with dark liquid. They both took a sip as Jill returned with a laminated menu for the two of them to peruse.

"Jill, could we just have a sandwich?" Steve asked, not even looking at the sheet in Mandy's hands. "You want anything in it honey? We do a lovely club sandwich with chips; would that be alright?" Jill said with a wry smile.

Steve nodded and Mandy chimed in asking for the same.

Jill returned with the sandwiches a few minutes later, they both thanked her. The food looked hearty and neatly plated. Four neat triangles of granary bread with stunning layer of chicken breast, crispy bacon and crunchy lettuce. On the side, was a bowl with salad and a little bucket of chips finished with a ramekin of ketchup.

Jill went to walk away but Steve caught her eye, "Everything alright?"

"Yeah, o'course. Looks like its picking up in here".

She quickly looked around the bar, "Yeah, It's picking up, should be packed later. I mean there's only two pubs in the village and the other one closed down ten years ago".

Steve chuckled at her words, he took a liking to her

sense of humour, she was young but came across as sharp and witty.

***

The bar was packed, so Jill had to move some tables to the side to make more standing room. The plates for Steve and Mandy's meal had long been cleared away, leaving only a few empty glasses. Another young woman stood behind the counter now; Jill was still helping but she was sitting with her father slowly nursing a pint of bitter.

The bar was alive, a jukebox at the end of the bar was providing a great atmosphere, playing a great mix of songs. The crowd was chattering and swaying in a way that invited even outsiders to join. As Steve finished the dregs of his drink, he looked at Mandy, "Another my sweet?" he asked lovingly.

Her face wrinkled with an inner turmoil, "I do want one, I'm just scared about the money though, we have already spent thirty quid".

Steve nodded, "Well let's just have one more then we can head off to bed". Mandy's face returned to a smile and she nodded her approval.

Steve arrived at the bar with their two empty glasses. Jill saw him and made her way over to serve him. "Another two?" she exclaimed as she took the glasses and popped them on the back of the bar. He nodded before he turned to look over the room. "I didn't think you would even fit this many people in here" he quipped.

Jill laughed, "I said we would pick up".

"So, are many of these staying with you?"

She had just put ice in the glass and held it up to the optic. "No. It's only you two staying here, everyone else lives locally." Steve went to say somthing but Jill continued. "These ones are on me by the way, Henry paid for a full meal and you only had a sandwich. Besides, he said you two were really nice and to look after ya".

Steve knew there was no point in arguing so he decided not to. He went to thank her when somebody in the crowd behind him cut across his thoughts. "OI, JILL! What happened to the music?"

Steve looked around, it was a young lad who barely looked old enough to legally drink.

Jill left the glasses on the counter, reaching over the counter side to whack the jukebox, the screen was awash with blue, error codes flashed across the screen. The thump she gave it did nothing to revive the music, it was cutting the atmosphere and people were moaning. She called out to the lad, "I'll come round and have a look in a moment".

She finished pouring the drink, her face now awash with annoyance. "Hunk of crap, that stupid machine." She muttered, handing over the drinks before walking around the counter.

Back at the table, Steve placed the drinks down upon the table. "What happened to the music?", asked Mandy.

Steve chuckled, taking his seat "The jukebox died, Jill is trying to fix it now".

Mandy grabbed her glass and took a sip; she was watching him carefully. Steve's eyes kept drifting to the stage in the corner of the room. They sat in a few moments of silence before anyone spoke again, "Steve, are you OK?" Mandy asked.

As soon as she had asked, he blurted out "Do you think that is in tune?"

This seemed to catch Mandy off guard, she stuttered and tried to see over the crowd in the direction of his gaze. As the crowd ebbed and flowed, she saw the battered piano on the little raised platform.

"The piano?" she enquired. Seeing him nod eagerly, she continued airily "Why do you think I would know?"

He didn't look back to her, mesmerised by the instrument he just mumbled "Just asking".

Mandy's lips curved into a smile, she recognised that look, "Why don't you go have a look?"

Steve's eyes lit up, as he looked towards her again, "You don't think Jill will mind, do you?".

Mandy again chuckled, "Well if she does, just get off of it".

Steve nodded and stood up eagerly, he took his drink and meandered through the crowd and onto the stage.

The piano was made of a beautiful cherry coloured wood, the tall back unit was a little tattered and stained with watermarks but seemed to be in working order. He lifted the fallboard covering the ivory keys, some of the keys were stained but again everything seemed in order.

He placed his drink on the back of the unit and brought down his index finger on one of the keys. A crisp note emitted from the unit and his lips curved into a smile. He pulled out the stool under the unit and cracked his knuckles before lowering himself onto the seat.

His fingers found the keys, the music echoed around the bar, filling every empty space with his beautiful sound. As he played, he set into a rhythm and began to sing, his voice was gritty, soulful, and powerful.

He was only singing a cover of an old song, but he made it his own. People stopped talking and the bar fell silent, all except for the magnificent blues cover he was playing. Eyes jerked in his direction; his voice was subconsciously commanding them.

The song reached its crescendo and he withdrew his fingers from the keys. He exhaled and reached for his drink, but a sound distracted him, someone was clapping. Suddenly applause roared from the crowd. He stood from the stool and held his hand in the air to thank the crowd, he grabbed his drink and turned to walk off stage.

"You can't just do one!" a voice shouted out from the crowd. Soon roars of "ANOTHER!" and "MORE!" were plummeting from the crowd. Steve hadn't felt this alive in years. "You want me to play another?" he called out to a rave reception of applause and cheers. He took a swig of his drink and sat himself down again before he obliged.

He played another two songs which the crowd received just as well as the first, he was enjoying playing but worried he had left Mandy too long. He stood again to calls from the crowd to continue, "I'll be back in a bit" he reassured them to another loud applause as he stepped down. He walked back over to Mandy who was smiling proudly, "How was it?" he asked.

She hugged him and patted him on the bum, "You sounded amazing baby".

Steve released her and went to sit down at their table, but he felt a hand on his shoulder. He turned round to see whom it was. The hand belonged to a middle-aged man in a smart white shirt tucked into dark blue jeans, short brown hair was over his plump friendly face. "That was great, can I get you and your misses a drink?".

Steve glanced at Mandy who was nodding gently and back to the man. "Thank you, two vodka and cola please."

"And what is she having?" he quipped, laughing at his own joke.

He turned to the bar where a young lady stood

looking airily into space, "Shauna!" he shouted, "get whatever these two want and one for me".

He turned back to Steve, "So what's your name?" he asked.

"Steve and Mandy"

"Well, Steveandmandy" He laughed again reaching out to shake his hand.

The pair just glanced at each other, not wanting to be impolite.

"You play really well, and your voice is just fucking… wow" he exclaimed genuinely.

"Well, I'm glad you like it, and what is your name" Steve asked, releasing his hand.

Before he could answer Jill swooped over with the three dinks on a tray, "Now then Paul, leave these nice people alone".

He looked at Jill incredulously, took his drink from the tray and wandered off without another word.

"Sorry about that" she said as they took the drinks from her tray.

Steve laughed, "He was OK".

Mandy chortled, "Come on Steve, he was a bit of a dick".

"Yeah, he was a bit of a dick, but harmless enough".

Jill laughed, "You're right, he is, anyway, don't

worry about him, I've just come over to thank you, are you going to play anymore?"

Steve was quite taken aback, when he busked he was often told to shut-up or move on but now he was welcomed, even encouraged to play. He simply replied, "I will if you want me to!"

Jill gleamed, "Excellent, the jukebox is totally dead, so I asked some of the youngsters in a local band to pop home and get their instruments. I didn't realise we had a musician here already. I'm sure they would be honoured to play with you, I mean they aren't that good, shit really, but desperate times and all that." She finished with a chuckle and walked back towards the bar.

Steve was positively beaming as he turned back to Mandy, "Ya can't say better than that! Bugger-it, I'll go and get my guitar".

Mandy kind-heartedly rolled her eyes, "I best ingratiate myself with the bar while you play". She grabbed his hand and walked him back to the bar where Steve bounded up the stairs back to the room to collect the guitar Henry had kindly bestowed upon him.

Mandy stayed at the bar nursing her dink chatting with Jill, she saw that a group of lads had entered the bar holding instrument cases, they stopped half-way into the premises and started chatting with Paul. He was laughing and pointing to the stage, the lads suddenly looked quite downcast. Slowly they made their way forward to the bar, "Jill, what's going on?".

Jill welcomed them warmly, "Lads, you're here!".

The young man holding the guitar case had a sour expression, "Yeah, we're here, you could have said you found some fucking nutter to play piano, we all rushed down here to help out".

Jill raised her eyebrow and her lip curled slightly into a menacing smirk, "Firstly, watch your fucking language with me boy".

He bowed his head a little and mumbled "Sorry".

Jill held her hand up to stop them from talking before continuing, "Secondly, you know you sound… ropey… to say the least".

The group of lads all looked a little defeated and tried to speak again but Jill held steady and continued speaking, "Finally, I have asked him if he would be happy to play *with* you, which he very kindly is happy to do. Now I am done speaking and will happily receive an apology for your little outburst."

The group all had cheered up immensely, they were visibly excited at the opportunity to play with an experienced musician so one by one they all apologised to Jill who had walked round the counter and gave them each a motherly hug as they did.

Jill looked around for Steve, but he hadn't returned yet, when something crossed her mind, she turned back to the lads who were ordering drinks with Shauna behind the bar, "Wait! how did you hear about the show earlier?".

The lad with a violin case spoke up nervously, not wanting to piss her off again, "Pete told us we weren't needed, you had a wild traveller guy here to play piano. Pete was saying he overheard the guy saying we were..." Jill's nostrils flared before he finished speaking. She shouted "PETE!" and she stormed off away from the lads to find him.

Steve laughed rather loudly causing everyone to jump. He stood next to Mandy holding his guitar case. The lads all looked a little unsure, but Mandy punched his arm jokingly, "Where the hell did you come from? How long were you standing there?".

He rubbed his arm smirking, "Long enough to know I'm a *wild traveller* and not to fuck with Jill".

The lads laughed nervously, but Steve held no malice, he was in a great mood, he held out his hand to the lads and greeted them friendly. He introduced himself and Mandy to everyone and asked what instruments they played.

Each in turn the lads replied their greetings and shouted out what they brought, "fiddle" "accordion" "banjo" "slapbox".

Steve thought for a moment, they had quite the

compliment with his guitar and the piano. He was muttering to himself quietly before he spoke again, "What songs do you know?".

The lad with the fiddle again spoke up for the group, "We know a few covers but it's a bit rough, we are better when we just kind of play erm… by ear. If you start, we will follow you." Steve nodded and pointed to the stage, "OK, sounds good, should we get setup then".

With that he led the way to the little stage in the corner and unzipped his guitar. He pulled out the stool from under the piano and strummed a few chords. He repeated the chords a couple of times then the lad with the slapbox joined in creating a baseline to the beat. Steve pushed on with the beat and started to sing a folksy cover of an old song that was popular many years ago. The accordion and banjo joined in on the verse and the fiddle came in at the chorus.

The crowd was watching them in fascination, they were cheering at the end of each song and crying out for more. Even Dave, Jill's father and his friend were watching intently. Each time Steve started playing, the lads joined in and created a beautiful melody.

***

It was past closing time but there were still quite a few people in the pub and the door was still open. Steve was talking with some people around the piano, as he finished his drink. As he finished the last of his drink he headed over to Mandy. She was sat down with Jill and some other ladies. "You alright babe" Steve asked Mandy magnanimously.

Mandy looked towards him, her eyes brimming with love, "Yeah I'm fine" she replied as she extended her arm around Steve's waist, pulling him in closer.

Steve leaned into Mandy's grasp, enjoying the physical connection with her, "What time do you normally shut the bar Jill?"

"Before three as a rule, but it doesn't really matter." She spoke dismissively as she took a sip of her drink.

Mandy was a little taken aback by this response. "Don't you ever get the police in?" Mandy persisted as Jill started to laugh.

"The police?! Around here? You're joking! There isn't a cop shop for miles."

Steve understood the implication, with no police there was nobody to enforce the licenced hours of the bar.

Mandy nodded, "Well that's handy!".

Jill laughed, "It's good for trade" she smiled, as she finished her drink.

Steve stepped away from Mandy and stretched, "Well I'm beat, I think I might go to bed".

Jill looked at him politely, "Oh, OK then".

Steve politely nodded before he turned to Mandy, "You coming?".

Mandy was laughing with the other ladies at the table, she didn't really look at Steve as she spoke "I'll come along in a bit".

Steve put his hand on her shoulder and gave it a little squeeze causing her to look towards him, he bent down to her ear and whispered "What about the bath?".

Mandy downed her drink and stood up purposefully, so much so she nearly knocked him off balance. "Night everyone and thank you for everything" she said warmly to the table before taking Steve's hand and leading him upstairs towards their room.

They headed straight into the bathroom, pulled the cord which sent light flooding over the clean, white bathroom suite. Mandy started to run a tub of steamy, hot water, liberally adding complementary bubble-bath from the sink unit.

Steve walked over to the toilet and unzipped his trousers to relieve himself. The sound of urine sloshing into the bowl drew Mandy's attention, "STEVE!" she mockingly scolded him. He looked around briefly, laughing.

Mandy stripped off, and slowly lowered herself into the water, Steve stepped out the room and returned naked, holding two of the large bath sheets. He placed them on the wall rack by the tub before stepping into the water himself. "Steve you've weed on the seat" she said, again feigning her disdain.

"Sorry I got distracted" he mumbled, leaning in to kiss her. She just giggled and kissed him back.

Steve and Mandy sat enjoying the warm water, relaxing their muscles and filling them with calm pleasure. They simply looked at each other lovingly. He was soaking in every inch of her beauty, basking in her radiance. She was lost in his wide eyes, so full of love and adoration.

Steve decided to break the silence first, "Did you enjoy tonight?" he asked. "Yeah, it was nice, Jill and her friends are very sweet".

"What were they talking about?"

"At first, they were all talking about you, but I soon changed that" she giggled.

"Just as long you were alright without me".

"Yeah fine, honestly it was nice to get away from you for a bit if you must know", laughing as she finished speaking.

Steve joined her with a rambunctious laugh, "We never did find out about the bus times, did we?".

"Actually, Jill offered to have her son take us, she said it was the least she could do for providing some background noise."

"*background noise*" he repeated incredulously, "cheeky mare!".

"Well… I was paraphrasing, besides that is what you pick up on? I'll try again, we have a ride tomorrow now."

"Sorry, yeah, that was good of her." He leaned in and kissed her again.

***

The morning sky was dull, grey and overcast, not that any light could enter the thick draperies closed across the large windows of the hotel room. Mandy shifted in the bed; the heavy duvet was keeping her warm and safe. She needed the bathroom, sleepily she wormed her way out of the cover, walking quickly to the bathroom.

She hovered over the pan and urinated, shivering slightly as she flushed the toilet and returned to the bed. Before returning to the warmth of the duvet she looked to the little clock on the sideboard, "Fuck!, FUCK! Steve!" Mandy rolled over to his side of the bed, and started to shake him awake.

"Mm, mm what"

Mandy had already stood up and started gathering things together, "It's nearly mid-day" she called to him as she was busying herself.

Hearing her words, Steve sat up quickly and rubbed his eyes, "Really".

"Yes, really!"

He jumped out of bed and started pulling on his clothes, Mandy was now dressed and stood with her bag by the door to the room. "You got everything?" he asked as he fought to get his coat on.

"I might have" she said winking.

Steve grabbed his bag and stood next to her, both scanning the room for any stray possessions. With the all clear, Steve said, "Right lets go" and led the way out of the room.

Mandy turned at the door and waved before whispering "bye-bye room" then followed Steve downstairs.

Jill greeted them both at the bottom of the stairs, "Good morning all, and how are you today?" Jill was very cheerful, she motioned to a table for them both, and walked onwards with the plates she had in her hands.

Steve and Mandy sat down at the table and Jill

returned within moments. "Let me get you some breakfast while you're waiting for your ride, full English? My treat."

Steve was taken aback by her generosity, "A full English would be great, but Jill you don't need to do all this, I mean it is appreciated, but you're too kind".

"No, I have already told you Steve, it's a thank you for last night, a lot of people stayed and spent quite a bit of money, it was the best day I've had in ages. So, you just sit there, enjoy your breakfast, and when you're ready will get you out of here" She nodded at them both confidently then walked off behind the bar.

The bar was getting busier, people were ordering breakfast and enjoying coffee. Jill stopped by their table after a few minutes bringing them two fully loaded plates, teas, and toast. Mandy and Steve looked at each other, large smiles on their faces, they winked at each other and tucked in.

***

Jill walked past their table and cleared the empty plates and used cutlery. Steve and Mandy rested back in the chairs as they both rubbed their stomachs. As she walked past they peppered Jill with compliments. She smiled at the praise they both offered but waved her hand airily, "You are both truly kind, thank you. I also wanted to let you know your taxi is outside if you're ready".

Steve led the charge by standing up and offering his hand for Mandy. Mandy took it and let him help her up. They both gathered their belongings and followed Jill outside to the car. Mandy opened the boot of the car for Steve to put their stuff in while Jill looked on kindly. When the car was loaded, she walked over to them, "Right, you two, come here!".

They turned to Jill and she wrapped her arms around them both and pulled them close for a tight hug.

"Thanks Jill, it was lovely to meet you", Mandy became a little teary as she spoke.

Jill embraced her again, "Well if you're ever in this part of the county again promise you'll come back and see us!"

Steve chimed in eagerly, "Yeah we will definitely come back this way one day".

Jill leaned in and gave him a hug too, "Well I can't wait!". She let go and stepped behind the taxi.

The driver wound down the window, "Alright mam?" he said warmly to Jill.

"Yeah, thanks for this Dan, and make sure you don't take any money off of them, this is on me".

"OK mum, no probs", and with that he started the car and drove off, leaving the beautiful pub to grow ever smaller in the distance behind them.

CHAPTER SIX

The car left the bus lane and pulled into the end of a taxi rank. The street was peppered with smartly dressed people walking swiftly, they had purpose and focus about their stride. Steve watched Mandy as she observed the passers-by go about their day as the car slowly reaches a stop. Dan applied the handbrake sternly and quickly stepped out of the vehicle. Steve joined him at the back of the car where Dan had already opened the boot. Steve started to hand some of the bags to Mandy and took his guitar case onto his shoulder.

Steve held out his hand to Dan and shook it warmly.

"Cheers then mate", Dan spoke magnanimously.

Steve smiled and replied warmly, "Yeah, nice to meet you Dan, and please tell your mum thank you again for everything".

Dan went to walk back to the car, he turned briefly and embraced Mandy, "Bye Mandy, take it easy" with that he returned to the car and drove away.

Alone now on the busy street, Steve and Mandy looked around and took in the sights and sounds. The streets, buildings, the people.

Steve turned back to Mandy, "Right then misses" he stated warmly.

"What are we doing first?" Mandy interjected. Steve looked to the sky as if looking for a plan written amongst the clouds.

His eyes returned to Mandy before he spoke, "We need somewhere to stay, there must be a shelter round here somewhere. I think we should try and find that first and then start afresh in the morning".

Mandy nodded her agreement, "If we look for a library or council offices, they should have some information".

Steve smiled at her, "Right you are, sounds like a plan, lead on".

They walked off in-amongst the people, the midday sun washing them in its beautiful warming rays. The tall buildings cutting into the sky above channelling them forwards.

Before them a large building lie at the brow of the hill, it was an austere stone structure that had bold columns either side of the steps, leading up towards the entrance. As they grew closer a large placard came into view, it was boldly attached above the doors. Finally, they were close enough to read it, '*Public Library*'.

Steve led Mandy into the building, the layout was breath-taking, it was in total contrast to the foreboding look of the outside. A huge glass atrium was allowing light to flood the building. A mezzanine terrace surrounded the main floor's reception desk, end-to-end with ceiling height shelves, shelves filled with a vast array of books. The roof also bore an array of chandeliers, enhancing the grandeur of the building and saturating even the furthest recesses with light. At the entrance, a seating area stood empty. Steve guided Mandy to one of the empty seats and placed his belongings on the chair next to her.

"I'm just going to ask for some information, I'll be right back".

Mandy beamed at him while she took a seat, picking up a stray magazine to read. Steve left her by the entrance and walked to the sweet looking lady sat behind the large oval reception desk. The woman had her black hair pulled back into a tight ponytail, and somewhat of a kind face, half hiding beneath oblong spectacles.

She wore an oversized striped knitwear jumper that

disappeared beneath the desk, enveloping her in wool. A lanyard lay proudly around her neck, terminating in an ID card displaying her name, 'Doris'.

"Excuse me, where would I be able to find some information about housing?"

She looked up from her screen, and smiled at him, "Good afternoon sir, of course." Lifting her arm, she pointed to the far end of the building, "If you walk through the archway, there is an office for the Citizens Advice Bureau, they should be able to help you".

Steve couldn't help but resonate on the way she addressed him, 'sir', he enjoyed being spoken to respectfully, it had been a good week so far, maybe this really was the beginning of their new start.

"Thank you miss, very much appreciated."

Steve bowed his head respectfully and started walking in the direction she indicated. He crossed the light-coloured parquet floor towards the far end of the building. As he got closer to the back of the building he saw a sign that directed him to a small counter in a recess. The counter was not manned, a sign placed on the desk instructed people to take a ticket and to wait for the number to be called. Steve pulled out a ticket from the dispenser and took a seat on one of the two plastic chairs outside the closed office door.

The rich mahogany door was sturdy, austere, but

not quite soundproof. A woman's voice could be heard inside, gradually getting louder, a child was screaming and crying erupted from the door as it swung open. The woman was unkempt, her hair was wild and face bruised. Her fingers were wrapped tightly around the child's arm as she dragged her forward. Tantrum in full effect.

The library was so quiet, the spectacle of the woman and child reverberated into every silent crevice in the room. The woman was furious, she was screaming at the girl, at the man in the office, "FUCKING CUNTS!" the woman screamed as she rushed to leave.

The man in the office was formally dressed in black trousers and a waistcoat, his hair was thinning at his crown and his hairline was receding. His face made him look older, dark circles hung deeply under his eyes.

His face was downcast at the woman's words, he tried to recover his complexion, but the fake smile he drew upon his face could not cover his despondency. He went to close the door, but he paused as he noticed Steve sat waiting.

He exhaled deeply, before he spoke, "Come on through".

Steve pulled himself up out of the chair, "Are you ok?".

The man was a little taken aback by the man's genuine question.

"yes, I'm fine, thank you." he replied, extending his hand to greet the man formally.

"My name is Dante, whom am I speaking to today?", he enquired warmly.

"I'm Steve, my wife is waiting in the reception area out front, we are looking for any information you can give us about homeless shelters in the area", he spoke evenly, taking a seat where Dante had indicated.

Dante's eyebrow furrowed, "Homeless shelters?" he repeated, "Are you newly homeless, what were the circumstances?".

Steve took time explaining their story so far, from how him and Mandy became homeless, the gambling, the scam, the journey, and the events of the last few days. Dante stared at him, following the ebbs and flows of the story. As Steve finished speaking, his mouth was open, astounded at the tale.

The room fell silent as Steve finished his story; Dante turned around to a folder on the back wall opening it on his desk. As he read, he remained silent but intermittently shook his head. He looked up from his paperwork, his expression grim.

He took a deep breath before he spoke, "OK! Well, I have some bad news, I really want to help you but there is at least a 24-week waiting list for housing and to be honest, you both are not a priority, or 'at risk' candidate for council accommodation. Not being from the area does not help your cause. All I can really do is refer you to a night shelter, we will get you on the waiting list but, like I said, it's a long list."

Dante looked glum but met Steve's eyes. Unexpectedly, Steve was smiling kindly, "A night shelter would be perfect, thank you".

This caught Dante off-guard, historically, when he could not help people, or told them what they did not want to hear, they yelled, swore, cried, became violent. Not Steve, not this man, he was warm, kind and grateful, even for unwelcome news. He struck him as an exceedingly rare sort, a genuinely good man.

"Thank you, Dante,", Steve said as he stood up taking the address of the shelter, leaving his other arm outstretched to shake his hand.

Steve turned to leave, but Dante called out making him turn back. "Steve, your best bet is to get a job and save enough for a bedsit, don't stay out on the streets, make sure you get to the shelter early, it fills up fast. Look after your wife, she sounds like a special lady, you need to stay safe. Get back on your feet, don't fall into the traps of drugs, alcohol or worse. Stay safe."

Steve was moved by his words, he walked up to him

and again shook his hand warmly, "Thank you, for everything", and with that he left the room.

He had on overwhelming feeling of warmth after his conversation. He returned to Mandy, taking a seat next to her to relay the conversation he just had.

"WOW!" She exclaimed, "Well, shame about the housing wait list but at least we have somewhere to stay tonight".

"Yeah, he said to get there early, so we should make a move, what time is it?"

Mandy looked around, "it's gone 3pm now, yeah let's go", she agreed.

Steve held out his hand to help Mandy up before helping her on with her backpack. He grabbed his own and the guitar case before leading her out of the library. In the street he grabbed for her hand, she placed hers in his and they walked down the street towards their destination, hand-in-hand.

***

They had been walking for just over an hour, following the directions written on the pamphlet that Dante gave to Steve. As they turned into a side street, they saw a large warehouse. The building was nestled in a little alley off the main thoroughfare.

The building looked a little dilapidated, the wooden facia was crumbling, rust scarred the corrugated metal panels around the roof. Pallets were stacked to the side of the entrance, past this, the alleyway opened into a large square where people had congregated and started to queue.

"I think this must be it", said Mandy. Steve nodded and led the way to join the back of the queue.

"There's a lot of people here, do you think we'll get in?" Mandy asked, quietly trying to disguise her concern.

"It is still quite early; they don't even seem to be letting people in yet", Steve tried to reassure her.

As they were talking, he noticed several people had joined the queue after them already.

"Well, we'll have to wait and see", she muttered to herself.

The people in the queue made them stand out a little, Steve and Mandy were well groomed, clean and in fresh clothes. Many of the people around them were not so lucky. Steve couldn't help his eyes from fixing on a young man in front of him, his hair was so matted, even the hat he had attempted to pull over himself failed to hide the tangled hair beneath.

He turned to Mandy and whispered, "Do you think we should give him some money for a haircut?".

Mandy looked around and spotted the young man, shaking her head.

"it can't be comfortable" Steve continued wistfully.

Mandy remained silent although a smile had invaded her sometimes stern face. It comforted her to see the humanity had not left the man she fell in love with.

People started to move slowly forward; the shelter had begun letting people in. The line moved slowly but before long the pair were at the front. A woman stood with a clipboard, she had waist length dreadlocks, clearly well maintained, that draped down to the waist of her high-viz jacket. She was young, maybe twenty, her face had an air of welcome, but her features were stern and unforgiving. Probably a volunteer, Steve thought.

"Names", she said bluntly.

Steve replied in his usual warm, lively tone.

She looked up from her clipboard, face still cold, "Have either of you been drinking today?"

"No", both Steve and Mandy declared together.

"Have you any drugs on your person or have you taken any drugs in the last 48 hours?"

"No", they repeated in unison.

"Have you anything on your person that may harm or be used to harm anyone around you".

"No"

She tore off the sheet and gave it to a colleague before she returned her gaze to the pair. "Right! Go on through, find a spot for the night. As you enter, your belongings will be searched. If anything you have said is to be found to be false, you will be refused entry and barred for 72 hours. You both look new here, keep to yourselves and watch your stuff."

Steve led Mandy through the doors, and as they both walked in, they saw a man in a high-viz jacket behind a table, somewhat blocking their way forwards.

"Hi folks, we have the right to look through your belongings to see if you may have brought in anything you shouldn't have. In the event of finding something uncouth you will be asked to leave; you may not return within three days!".

"That's fine", said Steve, placing his guitar case on the table for the man.

Steve helped Mandy take off the backpack and again placed it on the table with their other belongings. The man opened each of the bags, looking through each of the pockets in the satchel. After he rifled through them for a little, he zipped them closed again and handed them back.

"Everything seems fine, thank you very much for your co-operation, you may now proceed", he spoke with a friendly tone and a welcoming cadence.

Steve and Mandy walked through to the main floor as directed by the man's outstretched arm. The hall was vast and expansive. Filling the hall were rows of z-beds laid out in perfect rows on a parquet floor, creating a perfect grid that went on as far as the eye could see. The other side of the building, a servery was setup but not yet illuminated. The back wall had a closed set of double doors that was marked with a large sign above, '*Toilets & Showers*'. It was a lot to take in for the pair.

As they had been standing taking in the layout of the building, more people had entered. They had been walking directly up to beds and laying out possessions. Lots of the beds near them had started filling up, not many were left next to each other.

"Let's find a bed", said Mandy, pointing to the other side of the building where there were still a few unoccupied beds.

"Lead the way baby".

Mandy grabbed Steve's arm and started to lead on, "Come on Steve, quick there's two together there".

She rushed over to the two adjacent beds, she put

her bag atop the left bed while Steve put his bag on the right. As his guitar case touched the top of the mattress a woman slammed a torn and ratty carrier bag on top of the bed as she tried to push the guitar case off the bed. Steve managed to react quickly and grab the end of the case to stop it falling on the ground.

An older woman, in her late forties, stood aggressively holding the bag. She was wrapped in an oversized men's tweed coat; a massive neon pink taffeta bow adorned the right chest panel. Her hat and fingerless gloves were both a matching pink knitted wool. "Hay!, what the fuck!", she shouted out.

Mandy walked over and stood next to Steve, "Sorry but my husband was there first".

"Was he fuck BITCH!, I've been here for ages! Sins' yesterday! Yeah that's right bitch! I've been here sins yesterday!" she was raising her voice and repeating herself.

Mandy's lip curled but her demeanour was unchanged. "You just put your stuff there now", she persisted.

Steve rested his hand on Mandy's back, he tried to interject, "Mand, just leave it, yeah?".

The woman had a smugness come across her face, "Yeah MAN! Fuck off, do what you're told", she spat venomously.

Mandy swiftly dislodged Steve's hand and moved around the bedframe. She stood toe-to-toe with the woman. Mandy was taller and swifter than this rambling, aggressive woman. The woman shrunk under the Mandy's stern glare; she was furious yet controlled as she spoke. "For starters, it's Mandy! Now you may take your shit and get away from my husband's bed because I am going to let you. Don't be near us".

The woman was shocked, but compliantly picked up her bag and shuffled away muttering, "Yeah I'm going to find my own bed" she looked around, "Over there I think", still shuffling.

"I don't like it when you get like that Mandy", Steve said gently as he walked round and embraced her.

"Well, you're too soft with some people, so I have to be sometimes, don't I?" Steve frowned but remained silent, "Right! one of us has to stay here at all times, OK?"

"OK", he replied.

"Well last time we stayed in somewhere like this, loads of our stuff got nicked cos you wandered off, didn't you? Mandy's face was sombre as she spoke.

"It won't happen this time, I'll stay right here all-night now".

Mandy smiled warmly, "I've got to find the loos so don't go anywhere".

"Not going anywhere! Staying right here!" he jokingly repeated as he lay on the bed, watching her disappear into the area marked *'Toilet's & Showers'*.

Steve turned onto his side, facing Mandy's empty bed. People were wandering around quickly trying to find beds. Over the crowd of rushing people, Steve's eyes settled on a young lad laying on a bed ten or so rows down. He was laying on his back, staring at the fluorescent lamps hanging down from the ceiling. As Steve was looking at him, the lad turned on his side, locking eyes with him. Steve couldn't help but wonder how someone so young could end up here. As Steve's mind was wondering, he saw that the lad was waving, looking a little reserved. Steve waved back to him and smiled, suddenly, a loud crash at the entrance drew his attention.

"THERE NOT FUCKIN' MINE I TOLD YA, YOU ARSEHOLE", it was coming from the search table.

Three large men in high-viz vests ran to the front and escorted the person out, screams and profanities filled the cavernous room. Steve pulled his head back towards the young lad however his bed now stood empty.

"Hi", a shaky young voice mumbled.

Steve looked around and saw the young lad had

walked over, he was standing the other side of him. With the lad closer he looked even younger. He was skinny, almost malnourished and his clothes were tattered and dirty. His blonde hair was greasy and cut unevenly, in places it was long enough to fall to his eyes. The eyes caught Steve, they were still brimming with innocence, a faded green colour, which almost shone silver under the harsh fluorescent light. The lad adjusted his hat pulling it down further to try and hide the small cut above his left eye. He didn't know what could have brought this soul onto the streets, but he felt a deep sadness that this young man was here.

"Alright? I'm Steve", he finally managed to say, sitting up on the bed.

The lad didn't make eye contact, he stared at the ground as he spoke, "I'm Kase".

"You're a bit young to be in somewhere like this".

"You're a bit old!" the lad retorted defensively, still unable to make eye contact.

"'I thought that you would still have your mum, or your dad".

Kase stammered, still unable to make eye contact. "What about yours?", he asked reservedly avoiding answering.

"I'm old now", Steve said flatly. "They

passed".

Kase was paying close attention to the way the parquet flooring fit together, "Life is easier without parents" he mumbled absentmindedly.

"Do you have anyone?", Steve pushed gently.

"Life is easier now!", he repeated in response.

Steve could tell that Kase did not want to discuss the matter, he decided it was best to change the subject. "Do you spend a lot of time here?", he asked kindly.

"They fill up quickly here".

Steve worried that Kase was being despondent, had he upset him with his questions? He did not know how to talk with him, although he didn't seem to be in too much of a hurry to get away. He just stood examining the floor while Steve remained seated.

"Your girlfriend is pretty!" Kase suddenly blurted out.

Steve looked around, sure enough, Mandy was walking across the floor, returning from the bathroom. She had a warm smile and a glow to her; her face was a little wet from where she had splashed it to invigorate herself. Steve couldn't help thinking that she would almost float rather than walk, she was his angel.

"I tell you what, how about you show me around now my misses is coming back?"

Kase smiled and nodded enthusiastically. Mandy arrived back and waved at the young lad, "Hi". "Looks like you made a friend".

He smiled but refused to make eye contact.

Steve nodded, "Yes, Kase is going to show me around, if that's OK, of course". He waited for Mandy to nod before he stood up and leaned over to kiss her, "Lead the way".

Kase waited for Steve to stand up before he walked on, Mandy called after them, "Don't take too long".

He walked to the servery and pointed to the counter. "That's where you get soup, its usually soup. They will open soon". He put his arm down then started to walk again. This time, he led him through the door to the bathrooms. There was a corridor with a large sash window, men to the right, ladies to the left. He led Steve through the door to the right, it was a large open space, along the far wall was five toilet cubicles. To the left of the door, a row of sinks, mirrored with a row of urinals on the back wall. The left of the room was walled off, that opens into a section of unpartitioned showers and a changing bench.

"It's busy in the morning", Kase said before spinning on his heel and walking back out. He walked around the perimeter back to the front of the building. "Sometimes they have doctors". He again turned before Steve could talk and walked down the middle of the beds, back to Mandy.

"Thanks for the tour", Steve said warmly, gently placing a hand on his shoulder.

Kase shuddered and stepped forwards slightly, dislodging his hand, "It's OK".

"Any trouble baby?" Steve asked Mandy, trying to again change the subject.

"Not really, someone tried to steal your bed Kase..."

"I'll go find another one then, it happens all the time" he said flatly, cutting across her.

"No need, I told em' where to go" She smiled warmly.

"Where?"

Mandy laughed heartily, "I mean, I told them to piss off!". She patted the bed next to her, inviting him to take a seat.

For the first time Kase curled his lips into a narrow smile, "Thanks!".

Steve sat down on his bed facing them both, "Have you managed to find work?".

"No, I can't really read or write, nobody wants an idiot working for them" He had no tinge of emotion to him as he spoke. It was as if he had nothing but negativity throughout his short life, negativity that warped his self-worth.

Mandy seemed to share Steve's observation, "I don't think that makes you an idiot sweetheart".

"NO, not at all, but why is it you struggle?" Steve added on.

Kase just shrugged his shoulders and kept his eyes on the floor, "I didn't really get on with school".

All three of them sat silently for a moment, the silence however was interrupted by another loud shout, "KITCHENS OPEN, FORM A QUEUE, NO PUSHING". People milling around the building, laying on beds, all stood and started to scurry forwards towards the servery.

The trio joined the queue, waiting in line patiently, in silence. Finally, they reached the front, a man was ladling soup into disposable cups, another volunteer was handing out bread rolls.

"Are you coming back with us Kase, or do you have somewhere else you normally eat?"

"May I..."

"Kase you don't have to ask, come on" Steve interrupted, leading the three of them back to their beds.

As they arrived back to their beds Mandy spotted a girl buzzing round their stuff. She looked like an addict, she had track marks and multiple missing teeth. Mandy clocked her trying to open Steve's guitar case which infuriated her. "If you want to keep them two teeth in your head, get away from our things!" She shouted.

The woman saw Mandy approaching and scarpered. They all checked their possessions, luckily nothing was missing or damaged.

"You're a nightmare" Steve said, laughing warmly. Mandy just chuckled and nodded her head in agreement, moving her bag back under the bed and motioning for everyone to take a seat.

After a few minutes, Mandy decided to try and make small talk with the young lad, "So, how long you been coming here?" she asked in-between bites of her roll.

"About a year, yeah a year now" he said, tilting the cup of soup, savouring every drop.

Steve chimed in with another question, "Do you have many friends that come here as well Kase?".

Kase was using his finger to scoop out the last of the liquid in the cup, "No" he managed in-between licks, "I don't really speak to anyone, and you're the first people that have talked to me".

Steve and Mandy exchange concerned glances before Steve spoke again, "Well if you see us anywhere, here or out on the street, you make sure you come and say hello".

Kase nodded politely, he wanted to speak but another loud voice called out, cutting across him,

"LIGHTS OUT". He quickly shuffled back to his bed, and they settled into theirs. Moments later darkness flooded the room.

***

It was morning, Steve and Mandy had slept somewhat disturbed when someone approached their bed, shaking them slightly, "Come on folks it's time to go, we will be open again at four pm" Steve sat up sharply, the hall was mostly empty, the volunteers had started packing away the beds against the far wall. "Come on move, time to leave", the man repeated more forcefully.

Mandy stood up and straightened her clothes out before collecting her belongings. Steve looked around again and noticed that Kase had already left.

Steve and Mandy finally made it outside, the doors slammed behind them. "Maybe we overstayed our welcome", Steve thought.

"Right, where are we going first?" Mandy asked purposefully.

"I need a job ASAP".

"I'm going to the council to see if we can rush getting a flat, if not I can look around for a squat".

"Do you remember the big clock we passed

yesterday?"

"The Roundabout?" Mandy asked, a little taken aback.

"Meet me there at 3pm!"

With that, Mandy kissed Steve passionately and embraced him warmly. When she released him, they both walked off in opposite directions.

CHAPTER SEVEN

S teve stepped gently through the busy people rushing to their destinations. His eyes darted between the blank faces of the flowing crowd. People didn't make eye contact with Steve; again, he was almost invisible to them. His guitar case was resting on his shoulder as he looked around. He needed directions to a job centre. He had been walking for a while before he realised how tired his legs were.

Steve saw a bench and decided to take a seat for a moment. He was contemplating his next move when he was distracted by an intense and soulful sound. A woman was playing in the near distance, she was strumming away gently on her guitar. The sound was intoxicating, a melody that captured the very essence of his soul. It drew him forwards. It drew him towards her.

She was young and elegantly dressed, her hair was clean and drawn away from her face in tight braids. She strummed away and tapped the fret board expertly. The melody overtook him, making him forget about his aching legs as he stood watching her.

She had quite the crowd watching. Somehow this young woman had broken the bonds of everyday life and used her power to free people from the chains of their mundane lives.

The music was powerful; in it you could hear pain, longing, release, and freedom. Suddenly she came to an abrupt stop and called out her thanks to the crowd. She packed up her guitar in its case on the floor before she airily picked it up and walked away. Re-joining the crowd of people walking the pavement, going about their business.

Within moments the crowd had dispersed, the normal bleak pace had returned. Steve went back to the seat and rested his legs. His head was still reeling from what just happened. Suddenly, another sound pulled his attention, a clanging, metal scraping metal sound. A street attendant was busy wrenching open a bin in order to change the bag.

"Hello", Steve had a friendly inflection to his voice and cheerful expression, "Where can I find the Job Centre?".

The elderly man, draped in a yellow, fluorescent council jacket, looked at him disapprovingly. "Lookin' fer a job or just signin' on?" his voice croaked, and breath filled with the stench of stale cigarettes.

"A job sir"

"Aye boy! good lad, I reckon it be down road an' second left". The man slammed the door of the bin closed and walked off, holding the half full bag.

Steve gathered his possessions and followed the path the man directed. In the near distance he saw a building of brown-yellow bricks and distinctive signage. He powered forward and entered the building by the double doors.

The hall inside was largely open plan, around the sides there were boards peppered with advertisements. Towards the back, rows of chairs were aligned, most of them occupied. The left of the hall was cordoned off, desks lay behind glass screens, overlooking the seating area. The whole building looked austere, and the staff looked stern and unforgiving.

Steve began looking around the boards, multiple jobs were advertised requiring qualifications, experience or equipment. Nothing that he would be able to do or travel to. He would have applied for anything, supermarket, warehouse, labourer. Nothing!

Steve made to leave but before he made it out the door, he turned to a smartly dressed woman, "Where would I find a recruitment agency?"

The woman didn't look up from her paperwork but offered directions blandly. Steve called a quick "Thanks" before he walked back out of the doors.

Steve approached the agency and walked up to the reception. A thin blonde woman was seated behind the desk. She was speaking on the phone in a sharp tone. Her brightly painted pink nails curled talon like around the receiver, "Well, **you** didn't hand in your timesheets on time, it's as simple as that!", her voice was unsympathetic as she rolled her eyes.

"That's not my problem!", she huffed as she slammed the handset down on the phone. "Ugh", she muttered before settling her eyes on Steve.

The woman's beady eyes washed over him, from his unkempt hair to his guitar case over his shoulder. She pursed her lips, which were made even smaller by the obscene blue eye shadow she had caked on her eyelids. "And what do you want?", she said curtly.

Steve smiled through her disrespectful tone, "I'm looking for work", he said flatly.

The phone started ringing again, distracting the woman's glare. She placed a form on a clipboard and slammed it down on the counter next to a cup of short, branded pencils. "Fill this in" She said already picking up the receiver again before waiting for a response.

Steve started looking over the form as the woman rolled out a generic greeting to the person on the telephone. He wasn't good at filling in forms really, Mandy usually helped him with things like that. He wasn't illiterate, he just struggled and always made mistakes.

He helped himself to a pencil and started to write his name on the top of the paperwork, the woman on the phone waved her hand viciously, trying to get his attention. He looked at her and she was frantically pointing to a set of seats along the back wall, indicating he should take a seat.

Her face was angrily contorted as she spoke on the phone. Steve thought it was probably best to take a seat and keep his distance from this lady.

Her shrill and aggressive voice was filling the small office, making it hard for him to concentrate but he persevered, filling in what he could of the form.

It had been nearly an hour since he walked into the agency. A loud bang came from the desk, the woman had slammed the receiver down again. She stood up and called back through a door frame to a colleague, "Why are people so stupid?" She spoke with venom, "Why does everyone think I'm here to clean up their mess?"

Steve could hear chuckling coming from the other room as the woman sat back down, "Are you not done yet?".

Steve stood up and smiled politely to the lady, "I didn't want to disturb you on the phone, but it asks for address here…"

"UGH! don't tell me you're homeless!" she cut across him, words dripping with disgust, "No address, no job. We are a reputable agency".

Steve's smile did not falter, it wasn't the first time he had encountered such vulgar people. He placed the pencil and clipboard down and thanked her for her time before turning to leave. As he reached the door, he heard the woman mumbling about people wasting her time as she shredded his form.

Steve stood outside for a few minutes, thinking of what to do now. Hunger was biting him almost as much as disappointment. There was a shop opposite him, he didn't like wasting money, but he decided to buy himself a sandwich. He was feeling frustrated that he hadn't found anything, in his heart he didn't truly expect to on his first day. It still stung.

He still had enough time to look elsewhere before making his way back to meet Mandy. He walked back to the square he was sitting at earlier to enjoy his sandwich. Luckily there was a bench available. Steve eagerly sat and pulled the guitar off his back; it was starting to ache from carrying it all morning.

He rubbed his shoulder and eagerly opened the sandwich, taking a big bite in the middle of the triangle. It was his favourite, ham, cheese, pickle.

A voice, close behind, took him a little by surprise, "Steve?". The disembodied voice sounded meek and familiar.

He turned round to the source, behind him stood Kase, waving gently, face filled with trepidation.

"Kase! Good to see you!", Steve patted the empty part of the bench, motioning for him to take a seat. Steve took another bite of his sandwich as Kase walked around and awkwardly slid back on the wooden bench. Kase remained silent, observing the people walking past them.

"What you been doing today?"

Kase remained silent, now watching a pigeon waddling around the floor, pecking at scraps on the floor.

Seeing that he was getting nowhere, he changed tact, "Are you hungry?" he asked, holding out the other half of the sandwich, "Its cheese and ham".

Kase nervously reached his hand out and gladly accepted. He hungrily devoured his first bite, chewing methodically. "Thanks", he finally mumbled, staring at the ground taking another eager bite.

Steve smiled kindly, "How did you find me?".

Kase swallowed the last bite and ran the packaging over to a nearby bin, turning on his heels and returning to his seat, he was still avoiding Steve's gaze. "I didn't have anything else to do". He said flatly.

He pondered for a moment, "Did you follow me?" he asked, careful that there was no accusation hidden in his tone.

Kase froze momentarily, "Is that a guitar in there?", he asked.

Steve felt he was trying to change the subject, at least he was talking. "Yes, would you like to see?"

Kase nodded enthusiastically, finally turning to face him. Steve laughed genuinely, pulling the black case onto his lap and unzipping it in a smooth motion. The stunning instrument looked even better in the blaring afternoon sun. The deep red and black body positively glowed, almost as if it was creating a light of its own; in contrast, the rich mahogany on the fret was absorbing the light.

Kase's mouth was agog, his eyes were hungrily devouring every stunning detail. "Is it yours?" he asked.

Steve chuckled, "a good man gave it to me", pausing for a moment he corrected, "a friend".

"Can you play?" Kase asked, with eyes wide.

Steve picked up the guitar, letting the case fall to the ground, and placed his foot on it to stop it from blowing away. He threw the strap around his neck and aligned his fingers to the strings. Steve started to play the strings. C chord, D chord, roll on to an E.

He played the chords skilfully and quickly, the melody filled the space around them, Kase was enchanted by the music.

People passing by stopped walking, staring at Steve and tapping their feet. Steve didn't even notice; he was in his own world. His fingers climbing up and down the fret bar as he strummed away ferociously.

He was lost in the music; he did not even notice when somebody placed some coins in the guitar case by his feet.

"OI!", a voice called out behind the crowd, Steve didn't pay it any mind. "OI! STOP THAT!".

A man in a yellow hi-viz jacket was pushing through the crowd, a council logo adorned his left chest panel. He was a younger man with short brown hair. His face was contorted with anguish as he shoved people aside to get to Steve.

As the voice got closer Steve was wrenched back to his surroundings, even Kase's gaze was drawn away to the shouting man.

He was stood in front of the pair on the bench, "You can't busk here, you'll have to move on or I'll call the police".

Kase remained quiet but Steve laughed, "busking", he shook his head "I'm not busking, I was playing my guitar for my friend here" tapping Kase lightly on the shoulder, causing him to jump.

As he spoke, he realised a crowd had gathered Steve

thought they had gathered because of the man shouting. "I can put it away, it's not a problem".

"Maybe I should confiscate it!" the man leered, "Homeless scum like you, probably stole it anyway".

Steve was ready to reply but Kase spoke up first, "You can't take it, Steve's friend gave it to him" he spoke with such innocence in his meek voice.

The man simply laughed at this child-like reaction. "You leave them be or I'll report you."

"I'm sick of you booting off every five minutes like a little Hitler". Someone in the crowd shouted forcefully. It was the owner of a fruit stall the other side of the seating area.

"Yeah! piss off" someone else in the crowd shouted.

Steve took the opportunity to repack his guitar. He tapped Kase on the shoulder and they slipped away un-noticed in the kerfuffle. Once they got round the corner, out of sight Steve checked on Kase, he looked a little wound up. "That was weird!" Steve muttered, half to himself.

Kase just nodded silently, he was calming down but still had a frantic air about his body language.

Steve looked at the clocktower in the distance, "Should we go meet Mandy?".

Kase replied simply with a smile and followed him as he walked off the pre-arranged meeting point.

***

Mandy had asked for directions to the council housing offices when Kase showed Steve around the night before. She had written the directions down on a slip of paper. She dug in her pocket and retrieved it, skimming the instructions as she walked. It took her a little while to arrive at her destination, but finally, she was standing outside a grey, grandiose building with a clocktower mounted on a large rotunda. This was not just housing but the full council services office.

She located a door marked as '*public entrance*' and made her way inside. The inside of the building was grand, there was a marble floor and rich walnut reception desk. The ceiling was excessively tall with a large glass chandelier. Enormous paintings adorned the walls and mouldings were brushed with gold around the edge of the walls.

Mandy made her way up to the reception desk; she was greeted by a sombre looking woman. Her pristine white blouse made her pale complexion look even lighter, only broken up by an obscenely bright red, rouge lip.

"May I help you, madame?"

Mandy smiled at the formality, "I'm looking for some help with housing".

The lady nodded and knowingly tightened her lips, "Yes madame, the housing department is next door. Just head back outside and it is the second door on your left".

"Oh! Sorry! Thanks!" Mandy stuttered, as she turned around to follow her instructions.

She followed the lady's instructions and found another door marked '*Housing*'. She entered and noted the difference immediately. This room had gawdy carpet, dim fluorescent tube lights, cheap seating and a row of basic looking pine desks with glass panels shielding the staff.

This was more like what she expected, the seats were filled with row upon row of people.

She walked to the reception desk and gave the clerk her name, the clerk instructed her to take a seat and wait for her name to be called.

Mandy was sitting at the end of a bank of seats, there were many people situated around her. Mothers struggling with addiction, women that sold their bodies, young lads that used drugs, homeless people from shelters, and other people generally down on their luck.

Mandy waited for hours, name after name was called. Yet more people arrived filling up every seat. She kept glancing at the large austere clock on the wall, it was passed 1pm now, still no sign she was near to being seen.

A scream came from the front counter, a woman had two children running around behind her seat. She had been regularly shouting at them to sit down or be quiet. But this scream was something else. "CONGRADU-FUCKING-LATIONS, YOU JUST CASUED ME TO LOSE MY FLAT. IM GOING TO LOSE MY KIDS. ARE YOU PROUD OF YOURSELF? COW!"

The woman reached down and took off her high heel shoe and started battering the glass with it. The children were screaming and crying at seeing their mother in such a state. Suddenly two police officers entered the building just as the glass shattered. The police ran forwards and restrained the woman, escorting her out of the building. One of the officers returned for the children and took them out too.

The clerk came over and made an announcement, "Some of you won't be seen today as we have lost a counter".

Mandy checked the clock again, 2:45, "SHIT!" she thought to herself. It was getting to the point that she wouldn't be able to make it back to Steve on time. She stood up and shuffled out of the room to the street and rushed to get back to the clocktower.

***

Steve had been waiting with Kase at the clocktower for just over an hour; it was 45 minutes after Mandy had arranged to meet him. He was getting nervous that something had gone wrong.

Kase also looked nervous, pacing back and forth, "The shelter fills up quickly!" he said nervously.

"You can head on over, if you like" Steve said absentmindedly.

"I want to see Mandy is OK" Kase said more determinedly.

"Me too kid! Me too!"

Steve was walking around the clocktower, almost keeping alignment with the clock itself, rotating like and additional hand on the face. Finally, Mandy walked up to the back of the clocktower. Steve threw his arms around her and couldn't bear to let her go for a few moments.

"I'm sorry I'm late, a woman got arrested at the housing office" Mandy explained, "It was the best TV I've seen in years" she chuckled haughtily.

Steve seemed a little unsure "I was worried" he said a little sterner than he genuinely intended, "As long as you're alright, I suppose", kissing her lovingly.

"Kase waited with me, should we make our way back to the shelter?" Steve asked, seeing Kase pacing in the corner of his eye.

Mandy nodded, motioning for him to start walking.

"OH!" she paused, "How did you get on?"

Steve just shook his head and reached out for her hand, leading her away from the tribulations of the day. Mandy smiled when their hands met, as always; he made her feel safe, she made him feel loved.

CHAPTER EIGHT

Mandy and Steve laughed as they both filled each other in on their respective days, even Kase managed a smile as Mandy spoke about the occurrences at the housing office. They saw the alleyway that concealed the entrance to the shelter in the near distance.

As Steve led the way around the corner all their eyes locked on the huge queue of people waiting, "are we late?" Mandy called out, addressing nobody specifically, her voice shaking a little.

"It's about the same time as yesterday" Steve reassured, even though he knew that was not quite true.

Kase looked a little nervous, his hands balled up by his side as he followed them.

"Come on, let's get in the queue", Mandy called out, taking charge and leading the way.

They walked back past the entrance and followed the winding line of people back past the pallets and into the open square. They stood waiting patiently as the people in front of them trudged slowly forwards.

***

Finally, the trio reach the entrance, a stern man stood with a clipboard guarding the entrance. He held his and up to halt them as he allowed the two women ahead of them through.

"Right! Sorry we only have two beds left tonight", he called out into the remaining queue.

Mandy looked at Steve, her face drained of colour. "Steve!" she muttered, voice shaking.

"Come on through you two, Sorry kid!" He shrugged.

Kase started to walk away with the others that had been turned away, his face white as a sheet. Steve took a few steps after him and placed his hand on his shoulder pulling him back to them.

"It's OK, you two go in, I'll be alright out here," said Steve.

Kase wanted to speak but Mandy pulled Steve sharply to the side, "You don't have to do that, just let him go in. We can use some of that money to get a cheap room somewhere".

Steve shook his head, "I'm not wasting money on that", He kissed her passionately, "I'll be fine, there must be loads of homeless people sleeping out here tonight".

He went to walk away before turning back, "You best take this though", he handed her the money he had in his pocket.

Mandy took it, concern plastered on her face, she knew there was no point arguing but she did not like this one bit. "You better look after yourself, old man!", she said coolly.

"I'll keep it safe baby, I'll see you both in the morning, yeah?". He smiled as he reached out his hand and stroked her face with his fingers.

Another group of people walked around the corner and were approaching the entrance. The man stood at the door rolled his eyes, "Are you coming in? There are other people if not!", his voice had a tone of warning.

Mandy turned around and linked arms with Kase, "Yes we're coming".

He went through the checklist as with the other night before beckoning them through the entrance. Mandy stole one last look back at Steve as the man was slamming the heavy wooden doors closed behind them.

Steve stood looking at the closed door for a few moments, waiting for the people to pass. He was standing in the cold night air with his bag and guitar, feeling more isolated than he had in the longest time.

***

Mandy and Kase had just been given the go-ahead after having their bags searched. The hall looked even more full than last night. It looked like every bed was already taken, people had already started to queue to get their food.

Mandy finally found a bed that was unclaimed, "Do you want this one?", she asked him, worried he would struggle to find a bed on his own.

Kase shook his head, "I'll be fine".

"OK honey", she encouragingly tapped his shoulder and eased herself down onto the bed. The left leg was a little shorter causing it to rock slightly as she did. "If you need anything, come get me!".

Kase nodded and walked off, searching for available beds.

Mandy watched him as he walked the floor, zigzagging the rows of beds. Finally, he settled on a bed one row down, four over. Thankfully, she still had him in her eyeline.

She placed her bags down on the bed and walked over to him, "Let's get some food".

She led the way to the servery, he dutifully followed. When they arrived, the counter was sparce. They were the last two up, there was only one tray of food left. Really there was only one portion, but she was happy to share.

Kase joined her at her bed, and they ate together in silence. Mandy tried to have a conversation, but he remained unresponsive. It looked like his mind was elsewhere.

Once they had eaten Kase got up and returned to his bed, he laid down staring at the ceiling. Mandy watched him carefully as she also lay herself down, covering herself with the course linen, it felt cold tonight. Her mind fell to Steve, "I wish we could have stayed together", she thought to herself.

"Steve was getting older", she thought, "and it's such a cold night". She could not settle, not knowing he was OK. She hadn't spent a night away from him in years, not really anyway. She tried to visualise where he was, what he was going through.

"Hi there!", the greeting interrupting Mandy's thoughts. A woman stood at the head of the bed, looking down at her. She was dressed all in black, a blue lanyard around her neck. She was older than Mandy but still had youthful eyes, orbs of deep blue. Her hair was tied back in a ponytail like a blonde nest at the back of her head. She clearly wasn't staying here; she was far to neatly put together.

Mandy looked up at the woman, from her bed, "NO!" she exclaimed loudly, "Sorry, I don't do God".

The woman chuckled heartily, "Well that's ok, but I'm a doctor" she said, "Doctor Andrews", she reiterated, condescendingly raising her open hand to her own chest.

Mandy sat up, "OH!" she exclaimed, "Sorry doc, you just look like one of that lot".

The woman laughed again, "My apologies", she held out a hand to greet Mandy, "I've not seen you here before so I thought I would introduce myself, Do you have anything I can help you with?"

Mandy took her hand and shook it briefly. From the corner of her field of vision, Kase caught her eye. Mandy released her hand and waved at him. The doctor followed her eyes, "You have a little admirer, do you?"

Mandy chuckled, "My husband spoke to him yesterday, he hasn't left us alone since".

The doctor's face dropped a little, her face turned cold. "I can have a word with someone if he's bothering you".

Mandy waived off her words, "No it's not like that", she insisted. She thought for a second before speaking again, "If you do want to do some good how-ever, you can help get him in a flat or something", she raised her arm accusingly, pointing to Kase "HE, shouldn't be in a place like this".

The doctor looked a little taken aback, "That's not my job" she said belligerently.

Mandy shook her head disdainfully, "No! it never is with you people", frustration peppering her words, "Look! I think he's autistic or something, there's no way he should be on the streets, fending for him-self, he is too young, too vulnerable".

"Why would you say that?", she asked curi-ously.

"Go and see him, talk to him, he deserves a better life than this. You and I both know a kid like that is going to end up dead if he stays out here".

The doctor looked at Mandy coolly, considering her words for a moment, "Thank you for your time" she mumbled and walked away without further en-quiry.

Mandy sat down and exhaled loudly, she was ir-ritated by her surface level concern and lack of commitment to *actually* do some good. She had met many people like her before, they worked high pay-ing jobs and volunteered once a month to dim the gnawing sensation of guilt. Guilt for adding to the societal income disparity, for not doing anything that would really change people's lives. It disgusted her; besides, she was already antsy, worrying about Steve, she hoped he was alright.

Mandy was not paying attention to her surroundings, her mind racing with worries. She didn't notice that the Doctor had indeed walked over to Kase. When Mandy turned in her bed towards the young lad she was taken aback. The doctor was sitting on his bed trying to talk to him. He was ignoring her in favour of glaring at Mandy.

When she noticed this, she waved at him and offered him a thumbs up. His face softened slightly, and he sat down next to the woman on his bed. They both sat with their back to Mandy. They were sitting together for a few minutes before she got up and wandered off.

"LIGHTS OUT" a voice called loudly; it came from behind her.

Suddenly the room was dark. Mandy turned to lie on her back, slowly descending into a disturbed slumber. In her sleep, she didn't notice that Kase had stood up, she didn't see his bed empty, she didn't see him disappear through the darkness.

CHAPTER NINE

Steve had been looking at the closed doors for a while until the dusk started to settle in. He finally exhaled deeply and walked on to try and find some refuge. "I should have asked if there was another shelter" he thought to himself.

He decided to follow the other folks walking by, hopefully they would be heading to a safe place to sleep. He followed them through the square, and they emerged from the alleyway onto a busy street. There were several pubs lining the street, revellers were jovially chanting and excitedly chatting with one another while they queued to enter the various venues.

The people he was surreptitiously following suddenly stopped outside a closed shop, they laid down something from a bag and sat on the floor. They were not looking for a place to stay as he hoped, they were setting up to beg for money.

Spirits slightly dampened, he walked through the crowd and looked for a quiet place to pass the night by. The end of the road however didn't provide such a place; it opened into a wide shopping vista.

Steve stood at the corner for a moment, taking in the view. "You alright friend?" a disembodied voice spoke out in a friendly yet shaky cadence.

He looked around and there was an older couple sat on the floor, covered in several coats and a large blanket. It was the man who spoke to him. The pair looked a little more war-torn than himself, maybe ten or so years older.

"Hello", he called back, waving gently at them both. His eyes scanned over the pair, they were well covered and relatively clean, the woman had gloves covering her fingers, but the man did not. His fingernails had a thin crescent of dirt hiding underneath them. The man had brown curls of hair flattened against his forehead, it was poking out underneath a fitted beanie hat.

The man gestured to the floor next to them, "There's a seat available, if you want to join us for a minute" he asked warmly, his words mashed together with a thick Polish accent.

Steve smiled and accepted the offer, easing himself down next to them.

The man spoke again, "This is Andrea…", she waved as he continued "and mine is Greig".

Steve shook both of their hands and greeted them warmly, "You both doing alright?".

The woman replied briskly, "Cold night but we're alright" she swept her greasy hair back from her face with her gloved hand. "You new here?".

Steve nodded "Yesterday" he replied, "I managed to get the missus in a shelter, I'm out here tonight".

"Are you looking for somewhere to stay?"

Steve was watching the people on the other side of the road, a man walked past them without stopping. As he passed by, he dropped a coin onto their blanket. "Thank you, sir," they called out in unison.

The woman scooped the coin and pocketed it quickly. Steve rubbed his hands together, with the sun gone from the sky the chill from the darkness had become sharp, cutting him, like a knife to flesh. He warmed his fingers and pulled his bag closer, fumbling with the zip. Rifling through the backpack trying to get another coat. He pulled over a thick overcoat from the bag, "Thank you, Henry" he thought to himself.

The woman was watching him closely, "We sometimes stay over there", she pointed at the street opposite where closed shops lined a neatly laid pavement in a precinct. "Security can move you on sometimes, but they are usually pretty relaxed".

Steve looked over in the direction the woman

pointed, "Thank you" he said warmly.

He sat with them for a little while, he told them all about Henry and Jill at the bar, which they revelled in hearing. They also shared their own story with him, how they came to the country, how they decided to come to the city and how they ended up on the streets.

Eventually Steve scattered to get to his feet, "I got to piss" he muttered, making his excuses.

He said his goodbyes to the pair, picked up his backpack and guitar then walked across the road. He walked further into the street, past the closed retail units and coffee shops until he happened upon a narrow alleyway with bins scattered. He dipped down behind a bin, unzipped his jeans and relieved himself.

Emerging from the alleyway a moment later he rezipped his jeans, a tiny moist patch at his crotch was the only evidence of what he had just done. Opposite the alley was a recessed doorway for an electronics store, he scurried over and took a seat on the ground.

The wind had picked up, it was biting at his exposed face and hands. He tucked the guitar behind him, placing his arm through the handle, and placed the backpack on the ground under him to take the chill from the ground away.

He was watching the street, ten minutes went by,

and nobody had walked past him. He felt safe enough that he started to succumb to his tiredness. His eyelids drooped as he shivered against the bitter cold of the city. Moments later he had entered a disturbed and troublesome sleep.

***

Mandy was dead, she was lain out in a casket, a wreath adorned her picture. Her sweet milky flesh lay in front of him. The sensation of loss he felt was coming from the pit in his stomach, he felt sick with grief as he approached her. She was so serene yet tormented with lifeless closed eyes. Paradoxically, she did not look like she was asleep, he watched her many a night as she slept, guarding her from the evil in the night.

She was not sleeping, she was gone, forever.

Still, he had to see her, he ambled forward, heart racing despair setting in as if his very veins were a cast for concrete, flesh was stone. He stood by her side he caressed her face gently as a tear escaped his dark eyes. He retracted his arm, steadying himself on the side of the wooden box that held his love.

He was about to collapse, all was lost.

He felt his weak legs falter as they began to give way to the heft of his misery. Suddenly, he was held steady. Mandy sat up, eyes closed but body alert. His heart rate sped up, "What the fuck is going on?". As if in response to his question, her eyes open to glowing beams of light.

He felt a pain in his abdomen, a powerful stab of pain, now another.

His eyes opened from his nightmarish dream; two men stood leering over him. They were dressed all in black, their padded jackets bore the word 'Security' in glaring white embroidery. The man stood directly over him kicked his stomach again. "OI" he shouted, "This isn't a fucking hotel, piss off".

Steve struggled to catch his breath as the men laughed, it took him a moment to realise where he was, and more importantly that the dream world he had been stolen from was just that, a dream. He struggled to his feet and grabbed his possessions before scurrying away.

As he walked, he heard the men throwing more insults after him, "Homeless scum, vermin, waster, druggie".

He just kept his head down and kept walking on. The night was at peak, he noticed the dark hue in the sky seemed a little lighter. As he arrived back at the junction, he could still hear the bass of the nightclubs in full flow. The streets were mostly empty now, he looked across the road and it looked like Andrea and Greig had also moved on. It felt like it was time to move away from the area, he didn't want to be around when the clubs kick out. That many drunk people usually spell trouble.

He didn't really know where he was but he decided to walk away from the clubs, his hands almost twisted with the bitter cold and his stomach throbbing from the assault. Ten minutes later he discovered a more private looking area to rest, it was a shop on the corner of an alleyway. The frontage was painted black, and the windows were obscured but it was definitely closed. "A sex shop", he thought to himself.

He again eased himself down to the ground, securing his guitar strap around his arm and sitting on his backpack. He pulled the coat as tight as he could as shield against the brutal cold encroaching on him. His eyes darted to the street, as far as he could tell he wasn't visible in the recessed doorway, nor from the road at least.

In the cold unforgiving night, again he sat there trying to calm down, he was upset at what happened, "They didn't need to kick me" he thought, "And I don't look like a druggie".

Their harsh words pressed him almost as much as their boots, at his heart Steve was a good man. He didn't see the need for the darkness of the world. He remembered being young, when he had his life together, a home, a job. If there were people down on their luck, he always tried to help or at least stop and chat.

He stewed on the events for a while until again, tiredness crept upon him, stealing him away from the waking world. His eyes closed and he was gone.

***

Kase was feeling frantic, he lay on his bed in the Shelter. The doctor had come over for the first time since he had been coming to the shelter. "Why did Mandy send her here? Was she angry I was here not Steve? What if something happens to him? Would she ever talk to me again?" His mind was positively racing.

He sneaked a glance at her, she was laying on her back, just staring at the ceiling. He couldn't be sure, but he thought she looked mad. What was he to do, the lights flickered out, plunging the room into total darkness.

He tossed and turned, finding no peace in his mind. He was alone now with his demons, torturing himself about things that could be. He knew for himself how harsh the streets could be. The sound of light snoring was creating a chorus around him that fed his inability to drift off into slumber.

A new desperation came upon him as he lay staring at the dark celling, his leg ticking back and forth rapidly in his bed, a powerful urge to urinate.

He pulled off the thin blanket and stepped out of bed. He always slept in his clothes, so nothing got stolen, he had fallen victim to that too many times before. He crept along the dark floor, guided only by the mildly illuminated light above the door to the bathrooms.

He turned towards the gents and quietly hurried to a urinal before relieving himself. The sound of urine hitting the bottom of the porcelain filled the otherwise silent room. He squeezed out the last few drops and washed his hands.

In the corridor he paused, turning around he looked at the blackened sky through the large sash window. He felt a bad omen in the air, something wasn't right.

***

The nightclubs had all kicked out and the roads were temporarily engorged with people rushing to find food, taxi's, and lovers. The crowd thinned out within the hour as the black sky shifted ever so slightly to a deep blue, the sun is on its way.

Three lads had just been kicked out of a nightclub called 'Zanzibar', they did not hear the music cut off as they were in the toilets, all huddled into one cubicle. "C'mon Jack, get it racked up" one of them slurred in a whispered tone.

Jack was decanting white powder onto the back of a driver's licence, the licence belonged to the lad that was speaking, Andy. As Jack went to work separating the powder into three lines the third was busy fumbling with a fifty note, trying to roll it into a tight tube.

Jack was done, he wiped the edge of the debit card he used to divvy up the lines and rubbed the powder into his gums, "Fucks sake Mike, hurry the fuck up".

Mike handed the note over and they each took turns deeply inhaling the powder. As the last one was done, they each wet their finger and wiped the licence, again rubbing the remaining powder into their gums.

The lads all looked similar in weight, stature height and dress, all wearing a uniform of light blue, designer jeans, a white undershirt with partially buttoned shirts. With everything back in their pockets, they exited the cubicle.

They stated to head for the door "Hold up lads" Jack called out, "I need a piss".

As Jack started to move towards the urinals the bathroom door swung open fiercely. A bouncer stood there with a suspicious look on his face. The loud bang of the door slamming against the wall caused Jack to turn around.

"We closed fifteen minutes ago, it's time to

leave lads" the bouncer spoke barely containing his anger, he knew what they were up to but didn't want the drama, it had already been a long night.

"Yeah mate, just need a piss…" Jack stated as he moved forward, "NO, it's time to go, NOW" the bouncer insisted more forcefully.

Jack could see this guy was really annoyed, he couldn't afford to be arrested with the powder still in his pocket, so he bowed his head and complied with his instructions.

When the lads got outside, and safely out of ear-shot, they started talking how they should have knocked him out and boasting how powerful they were, as they all agreed with each other and drunkenly rambled on.

There was a young woman waiting outside a takeaway, she was alone and was dressed in a black and silver shiny dress, her blonde hair falling down in loose curls by her shoulders. Her face was painted beautifully, accentuating her features.

Jack saw her and walked across the road towards her, paying no mind to the traffic, causing one car to slam on its breaks. He turned to it and punched the bonnet in outrage, "Watch where you're fucking going" he called out. The driver just waited for them to pass before driving on, deciding it wasn't worth the fight to stop or call out the behaviour.

The young woman saw this and rolled her eyes, she

was a little drunk, interested in getting home, in getting some food, and in getting to bed. She was not however, interested in him. She silently prayed her taxi would hurry up and arrive, so she didn't have to talk to him. Sadly, she was not that lucky.

"You alone there beautiful?" he called out to her, louder than necessary. Jack like the theatre of the chase. She shook her head and looked away to the road.

"Don't be shy" he chortled.

His arm went to fold around her, hand reaching to touch her bum. She looked really uncomfortable, luckily a woman inside the takeaway called over to her, "Is your taxi here yet?" she asked, "Come wait inside with us, OK". The woman gladly accepted and turned on her heels and rushed inside away from the trio.

"Fuck" Jack shouted, "Back to mine for some more beers them lads?"

The other two responded with a roar of applause, "Yeah and don't worry about her anyway, she looked like a frigid bitch!" Mike added.

They all laughed and followed Jack as he turned left, away from town at the crossroads. "Fuck, I really need a piss, I'm just going to duck into this alley" he pointed to a little alley with a black painted building on the corner.

He ran forwards leaving the other two behind but stopped as he arrived at the alley. He waved his friends over and was barely containing a laugh. He held his finger to his mouth signalling Andy and Mike to be silent. As they entered the alley, they saw why he stopped. There was an old man asleep in the doorway, he was sat on a backpack and his head was comically lolled forwards.

He pointed at his eyes and then at himself, signalling them to watch him. He walked closer to the man, turning again to signal to his friends to remain quiet barely containing his own laughter.

He straddled the man's legs and unzipped his blue jeans, taking out his dick from the black designer boxer's underneath. He stood for a moment aiming his cock before releasing a stream of steaming piss. The piss landed directly on his head, dripping both down the back of his clothes and forwards down his face, chest and torso.

The lads could take it no more and burst out in hysterical laugher which Jack joined in as the man came round.

***

Steve was in a room; the walls were painted magnolia with pictures adorning the walls. Pictures of himself and Mandy. He recognised this place, it was their house, the house they had once, the house they lost.

On their old sofa, Mandy sat down, she had a concerned look on her face, "We can't afford it baby" she muttered.

"As long as we have each other we have everything we need" he tried to re-assure her.

"It's all my fault" she screamed as she started crying, "I have ruined us".

He took a seat beside her and held her as she sobbed. "It's going to be OK" he whispered, stroking her hair.

Suddenly the ceiling started dripping, water was flooding the room, had a pipe burst? The room was filling with water, the picture frames fell off the wall and started to bob up and down in the water.

As the water level rose, he started to panic. Mandy continued to sob even as the water lever engulfed her, leaving her submerged.

He suddenly came back to consciousness, the dream clouding his reality momentarily. He felt wet, was it raining or was it just the vestiges of his dream still clouding his senses.

The sound of laughing cut through the haze, he looked for the source, there was a shape standing over him. It was a young lad, maybe twenty years old, dressed in blue jeans and a half unbuttoned grey shirt.

Directly in his eyeline was the lads exposed penis, urine flowing urgently from his foreskin onto his face and chest, "WHAT THE FUCK!!!" Steve screamed, fighting to stand up.

"What?" he asked innocently, stepping back laughing, "I'm just giving you a wash mate, what's the problem?"

"You were pissing on me you prick" Steve retorted, warm urine still soaking his body.

"What did you call me old man?" he asked, voice laced with danger. He finished up and zipped up his fly before leering closer towards Steve. He spoke again more menacingly, "Who's a prick, you old arsehole!"

Steve could feel the liquid quickly getting cold, he realised his bag was near a pool of piss, he turned his back to the youth so he could move the bag away to a dry patch. He didn't want all of his clothes to be contaminated.

As Steve stood up with the bag in his hand, he heard the lad shout something, "Fucking tramp! have this!"

The young guy punched Steve in the back of his head. The blow knocked him forward into the shop door and down to the ground. He was seeing blasts of white in his vision and he was on the brink of losing consciousness.

"Fuck him up mate" one of the other lads called out. This served its purpose to incense the attacker.

"Come on old man, what did you say?" he kept repeating, towering over his collapsed body on the floor amongst the piss and filth.

The man crouched down and grabbed Steve's head, pushing it firmly against the door of the shop. Steve quickly regained his faculties and pulled back his fist and punched him. His fist contacted his lower jaw, knocking him back on his arse, he was lucky and caught the guy off guard.

The other lads stopped laughing quickly and rushed forwards to help their friend. They provided a barrage of kicks and punches while their friend tried to recover his balance. There was nothing he could do to defend himself other than to curl up into a ball and cover his head.

The pain seared his body. Luckily, they were drunk enough to be sloppy with their aim, giving Steve a brief relief but he felt himself on the verge of losing consciousness again. The boy on the left who was less enthusiastic about the beating tapped his mate on the shoulder. He had noticed the guitar case, "What's this?", he asked tauntingly, "What have you got here?" the other repeated.

The first attacker had managed to get to his feet, spurred on by his mate's words, he tried to grab the guitar. Steve tried to hold onto the case, forcing himself to stay conscious, pouring all his energy into holding onto it.

The lad was enraged with his defiance, he let go of the case and raised his boot, bringing it down mercilessly onto his head. At this Steve lost consciousness and went limp. He grabbed the case effortlessly and laid it carefully on the ground to open it.

"A tramp shouldn't have this" he called out to his accomplices, bending down and laughing.

"Come on Jack, leave it now, we need to get out of here" the more reserved lad said looking around, watching out for witnesses or the police.

"NO" he demanded, "Trash needs to know it's place".

He slapped Steve heavily, trying to bring him round, after a few strikes he started to wake. The other lad had backed off and was watching him intently, a cruel smile plastered on his face.

He stood up admiring the guitar, "Probably stole this didn't you!" he accused bending down to grasp the instrument. He had it in his hand. He pulled it into the air and firmly slammed it down to the ground. The noise was otherworldly, haunting and piercing. The lad pulled it back again and brought it down to the concrete floor.

Steve was devastated, "No" was all he could meekly utter, reaching out a limp and bloodied hand.

The lad didn't stop until the instrument was nothing more than mahogany and oak scraps on the floor. He was ready to give back into the circling darkness of unconsciousness, a new sound stopped him.

Footsteps running towards them, an ear-piercing scream, shouting, footsteps running away. It was over in a moment. Steve came out of the ball and tried to sit up. His ribs were in agony, his hands were lacerated and bruised, and his nose was broken. There was blood and piss all over his coat, it was totally ruined.

The first thing he saw was the devastating sight of the shards of guitar scattered around the floor. Secondly, he saw that the two lads had run off, only one attacker remained. He was shrieking and covered in blood, not just flecks of Steve's but a river of his own.

Behind him was another figure, it took him a moment to realise there was anybody there, it was someone he recognised. It was Kase.

Kase stood there calmly, holding a long sharp screwdriver, dripping with blood. The man had collapsed to the floor grabbing his back, screaming with fear, eyes dilated with pure terror.

Kase stood watching him writhing on the floor for

a while, expression blank. He turned to Steve and smiled politely, "You alright Steve, just came to see if you were OK" he said nonchalantly.

Steve was a little taken aback, "Yeah I think so" he spluttered, taking a deep breath before trying to stand up.

He made it to a standing position, but he was unsteady, wobbling uncertainly. He was using the door to support himself for a moment. Kase watched him intently, ignoring the pleading and begging from the young man on the floor. "Please don't kill me" the lad shouted.

Seeing Steve was up and walking Kase said "Well, I'm going back then, night!". He bent down to the lad who flinched desperately. He held out the screwdriver, wiping the blood off on the lads blood spackled grey shirt before pocketing it walking off into the night.

The lad now crying and muttering incomprehensible babble, rolled on the ground in agony. Steve slowly gathered his possessions, bending down at the splinters of the guitar to mourn the loss. He examined the blood splattered coat, luckily against the black fabric it was invisible. He picked up the guitar case and eased on the backpack, making him wince in pain with each movement.

Ready to go, he looked at the boy on the floor, even with everything he had done, he could not leave him like that. He bent down over the lad causing him to whimper pathetically. "Please, I'm sorry!" he kept repeating.

Steve just shook his head disapprovingly and ignored him. He patted down his pockets and reached into the left-hand side. He pulled out a wallet and a baggie with white powder in it.

"Take it, please just help me" he begged.

"I'm trying, now calm down."

He discarded it on top of his chest before reaching into the other pocket and pulling out an old mobile phone.

Steve opened the phone and dialled the emergency services, "Ambulance please" there was a short silence before he continued, "There's a lad been stabbed in the centre by..." he looked up and read out the name of the shop. The operator continued asking questions, but Steve had no intention of sticking around. He wiped the phone off fingerprints and threw it on the ground, out of reach of the lad.

He stood up and took one more look at the man on the floor, before walking off, leaving the lad crying in the middle of the alley. He walked for ten minutes before the sound of the two tones in the distance started getting nearer.

The night was passing, the daylight was winning

the battle, warding in the new day. Back on the road with the nightclubs he was transported into another world. Street sweepers were busy cleaning the evidence of the night before, kebab boxes and chip wrappers were collected and hidden from the world of daylight.

He retraced his steps and walked back to the shelter. Not wanting to be seen, he stayed back from the entrance a little. He stripped off the coat and put it in the bin next to him before taking a seat on a stack of magazines located next it. His mind raced with the events of the evening. So many questions; "why did that lad piss on me? why did they break the guitar? how are people so nasty? how did Kase find me?"

With the last question he paused, "Wait, how did Kase find me" he asked himself. He sat there pondering as the sun rose in the sky, not daring to drift off again. The only certainty is the night would have been easier with Mandy, he missed her, "Not long now", he thought.

***

Kase looked at the dark night sky through the sash window, the feeling of foreboding grew in him, like clog in a river, he felt like tonight the banks would burst. He stood there until the fear of inaction overtook everything else he feared.

He knew what he must do, he tried the window, but it was screwed shut. He pondered for a moment before reaching into his cargo trousers pocket. He retrieved the screwdriver he had taken from his last foster home, all of them months ago.

Using the edge of the blade he managed to unscrew the four fasteners that sealed it closed, freeing him to explore the night. He knew above all else he must not get caught; he must find Steve.

He put the blade and the screws back in his pocket and lowered himself out the window, it was only on the ground floor, it wasn't a big drop.

Outside, he wandered off, in the direction he saw Steve walk earlier. He walked down side-streets and regular haunts for the homeless he knew of, nothing. No sign of Steve anywhere.

After a few hours he was giving up hope, he was also getting tired. As he walked to the last place he could think of, he saw a pair of familiar faces huddled up in an alleyway.

Andrea and Greig were sat covered in their blankets Grieg had his arm around Andrea who was sleeping soundly. "Hello lad" Grieg whispered quietly, not wanting to wake her from her peaceful slumber. "You're usually in that shelter, aren't you?".

Kase nodded, "I am" he answered plainly, "I'm looking for Steve" he added bashfully.

Grieg laughed, "OK, and who is that?" he asked.

"Steve is Mandy's husband" he answered truthfully.

"Hold up" Greig said, a little too loud causing Andrea to moan in her sleep. He lowered his voice and continued, "We met an old lad named Steve tonight, I'm sure he was talking about a Mandy".

Kase became excited, "Do you know where he is?".

Greig shook his head, "We said to bed down in the shopping precinct, but if he has been moved on, I've no idea, sorry kid".

Kase turned round and motioned his thanks before rushing off.

When he arrived, he searched the precinct but there was nobody there. He sat down for a moment, trying to clear his head. He was watching the sky as he sat, there were no clouds, the colour had changed, he could tell sunrise was not too far away.

As Kase was sitting watching the sky he froze, he was sure he heard someone shout in the distance, it sounded like 'What the' or 'When you' but it was something. He stood up rushing across the crossroads and on down the road. From afar, he spotted two figures, they didn't look like Steve, so he slowed to a walk. It was another false hope. "Maybe I should head back" he thought to himself, yet something compelled him to keep moving forwards.

Suddenly the figures disappeared into a side road, there were sounds of a struggle and then an almighty bang, an explosion of wood exploding into the silence of the night.

Kase hurried forwards, from corner of the alley he saw the three lads focused on Steve who was on the floor balled up, reaching for his prized guitar. The lad was standing holding the fretboard, smashing it into thousands of shards.

Kase did not like bullies, he had spent much of his life on the wrong end of bullies. Without really thinking he retrieved the screwdriver from his pocket, braced himself and ran forward, plunging it into the lads back.

The shriek was unnerving, it took Kase by surprise, he instinctively jumped back, pulling the screwdriver with him. There was blood dripping from the screwdrivers end and pouring out from the lad.

The sight of this was clearly too much for the other two as they bolted from the scene at the explosion of scarlet.

Kase asked if Steve was OK. When he heard Steve say he was, he was relieved. As Steve was looking at his ruined guitar Kase approached the lad and used his shirt to wipe the tool and his hands. The man cowered and whimpered as he approached, writhing to try and get away pathetically.

When he was satisfied Steve was stood up and safe, he excused himself and made his way back to the shelter.

He tried the window which slid open with ease, he managed to slither back inside silently. Before re-sealing the window, he nipped into the bathroom which was unoccupied and washed his hands, the screwdriver and any splatters on his trousers.

All clean, he screwed the window closed again, sheathed the tool in his pocket and returned to his bed. Sleep came easily this time, everyone was OK.

CHAPTER TEN

She woke with a start, sweat lacing her brow. She sat bolt upright in the temporary bed; she had a strange feeling of foreboding. She looked over to Kase who was dead asleep in his bed, his face angelic and peaceful. Her sleep was disturbed with nightmares, nightmares of the reality she now faced.

She struggled to be without Steve, how could she be so dependent on him, try as she did, she couldn't remember a time when she hadn't had Steve to pick her up and put her back together. Her nightmares filled her with dread. A world where she waited for him and he didn't return.

Not because he had found someone else, she could handle that, but he could not return because he was trapped, dying somewhere. It was a similar nightmare that she had, he was calling out for her; pinned amongst wreckage, trapped under water, falling from a great height. He was scream-ing for her, "Please Mandy! please help me! Save me Mandy!".

She could hear the calls for help but no matter where she looked, he was nowhere. She was left, trapped herself. While he needed her, she could not move on. She was trapped, tethered to him as if they were always teetering on a knife edge.

She threw back the sweat drenched sheets and stood up, it was clearly early, many of the beds were still occupied with sleeping bodies. A few people milled around by the bathrooms; hair wet from the shower. She gathered her own possessions and walked towards the bathroom.

She entered a cubicle and relieved herself, when she exited, she washed her hands, hanging the back-pack on one of the pegs provided. She stripped her-self naked and entered the lukewarm water. She scrubbed the pain of her thoughts, her nightmares away.

She stepped back and dried her body changing into new clothes from the backpack, "Thanks Henry's dead wife" she thought. She observed herself in the mirror, she looked like a part of society again, it helped alleviate some of the fears from her night-mares.

The room was starting to pick up, women swarmed about the room, washing and cleaning themselves.

She repacked her possessions and made her way through the groggy crowd. Most people were awake now, shuffling about their day. She glanced over to Kase; he was still fast asleep.

She returned to her bed and started to fold up the sheets neatly, busy work to occupy her. She wanted to let Kase sleep as long as he could, he looked like he needed it. She hoped nightmares hadn't kept him from peace like they had her.

She sat on the folded bed and waited. A woman walked closely by her bed, causing her to look up. It was a woman she recognised; her hair still tied up in a nest of blonde. She was wearing a blue maxi dress with white flowered patterns; a little black cardigan covered her shoulders.

It was the doctor from yesterday evening, "May I sit down?", she asked kindly.

Mandy looked up at her, she was inclined to tell her to piss off, after all, she was already too worried about Steve to deal with her nonsense. Something in her face made her reconsider. "OK" she replied curtly.

The doctor politely moved the folded sheets back a little, picking them up delicately and setting them back. "Thank you" she said kindly, lowering herself next to Mandy. "My name is…"

"Doctor Andrews", Mandy finished her sentence.

Her brow furrowed a little, "Gloria Andrews" she corrected, "Please call me Gloria" she added.

A little taken aback at the informality, she nodded, "I'm Mandy" she eventually added.

The doctor sat silently watching her for a moment, "when you saw me yesterday you didn't like me, did you?" she asked with surprising warmth.

Mandy let out a little giggle, "I can't say I had an opinion" she lied.

Gloria smiled kindly, "you must have met many people like me, a bandage on a severed arm", she looked at the floor, "I volunteer here one day a month to alleviate the guilt."

Mandy didn't know what to say, why was she confessing this to her?

"I see people struggling, I see homelessness, addiction, abuse, and I don't help, I can't help, it's just too much for one person to fix. When I go home, I don't think about the people here", she confessed. "It's not that I don't care, but by coming here and volunteering the guilt is kept at bay."

The doctor paused, bringing her gaze back to Mandy, "How do you know that lad? I mean really".

Mandy was puzzled, "Like I said, my husband talked to him, he just kind of latched on".

She looked at Mandy quizzically, searching her features for a sign she was omitting something. "And even though you didn't know him, you wanted me to help him?"

Mandy was getting annoyed now, "Yes" she hissed, "He doesn't belong on the streets, I don't need a degree to see that" taking umbrage with the line of questioning.

The woman exhaled deeply, "I'm sorry" she offered genuinely. "I mean no offense, nor am I trying to insult your intelligence. I was just really moved", she shifted uncomfortably on the bed. "Another thing you're right about, is that lad shouldn't be out on the streets".

She raised an eyebrow at the doctor's words, they brought a smile to her face.

"I wasn't lying when I told you 'I' couldn't do anything, but I've set up an appointment with someone that may be able to." She looked deep into Mandy's eyes. She was a rare soul, beautiful, caring, rich in ways she could only envy.

"An appointment?" Mandy asked enthusiastically, "Where? When?" she asked.

The woman laughed, enjoying the change in demeanour, "There's no guarantees but today! here! 5pm! I have arranged to use the office for some privacy, please make sure he is here on time".

Mandy stood up and faced the woman, "What brought you back here today?" she asked, careful to not sound accusatory.

"In all honesty, you did" she stood to face Mandy, "when I got home last night, I couldn't stop thinking about the way you were looking out for someone you barely knew; especially as you were also in need. It was breath-taking. I couldn't stand idly by".

Mandy stepped forward and hugged her, she reciprocated, "Thank you Gloria".

Gloria released her and blinked away the moisture on her eye, "So I'll see you both at five?"

"On the dot"

Gloria replied with a smile and walked towards the entrance.

"TIME TO LEAVE PEOPLE" a booming voice called out, echoing through the hall.

Kase jumped out of his bed, looking around, slight fear on his face. He locked eyes with Mandy and hurried over to her.

She greeted him warmly, "Morning Kase", she rested her hand on his shoulder, "Let's go find Steve".

He nodded and went to lead the way.

Remembering, Mandy called him back, "Oh, and we have to be back here by five tonight, I need you to come to appointment with me here", she didn't want to scare him by telling him too much.

"OK Mandy" he said proudly.

"Right then, lead on", she said, pointing to the entrance.

CHAPTER ELEVEN

An odd sunbeam danced its way through an overcast sky, coming to a rest on Steve's face. He was half asleep, half daydreaming, his eyes not focused on anything particularly. His head was pounding, and his ribs were cramping agonisingly. The sky making one thing clear, morning had arrived.

Around the corner the sound of heavy wooden door slammed back against the brickwork. The jarring sound roused Steve from his thoughts. He slowly eased himself up, fighting against the throbbing in his ribs. He walked towards the sound, leaning slightly against the wall.

A stream of people walked past him, some watching him suspiciously, unwilling to make eye contact. He paid them no mind, inhaling deeply before stepping around the corner.

Mandy was standing with Kase, she was looking

the other way, looking out for him. Kase spotted Steve and tugged reservedly on her coat to draw her attention. She glanced at Kase and followed his arm to see what he was pointing at. She clapped eyes on him, and her serene face dropped and contorted with horror.

He walked back away from the entrance, wishing to stay out of view of the volunteers. Mandy quickly followed him with Kase trailing slightly behind.

"Steve!" she shrieked in a whisper.

He just looked at the ground, a little ashamed. "It's not as bad as it looks", he mumbled, pre-empting her words.

She placed her hand on either side of his face, forcing him to look at her so she could examine it. Tears formed in her hardened eyes, she tried to fight them back but one streaked down her face, silently dropping to the floor.

She steeled herself before she spoke, "What happened?".

Steve did not reply, after all, what good would it do for her to know the events of the night. What good would it do for her to hear how Kase saved his life, she would only have another thing to worry about.

"I'm taking you to the hospital" she called out sternly.

"No! I'm..." Steve started to protest.

"NO, we're going, NOW!!", Mandy cut across him, grabbing his hand and walking towards the street. She walked briskly but slow enough for him to hobble along next to her. Kase lingered behind them, he was unsure of himself but decided to follow until they told him to go.

They emerged onto a street, smartly dressed people looked at him as a grotesque entity, with some even crossing the road to avoid him. Neither of them paid it any mind, it was nothing new to them, the last few days of blending into society had been nice but that was apparently over now.

Steve was struggling to walk, luckily Mandy saw what she was looking for, a taxi rank. Uniform black cars were lined up, waiting for a fare. Mandy opened the side door "Jump in Kase and help him in". He sprung compliantly into action.

They managed to help Steve into the back of the car. Safely seated, Mandy slammed the door and got into the front of the vehicle "To the hospital" she commanded sternly. With a nod from the driver, the car pulled away.

Steve was in considerable discomfort during the ride; he shifted painfully in his seat which wafted a faint smell of piss around the car. Luckily, most of it was on his overcoat which he discarded earlier.

Suddenly a thought crossed his mind, "Kase" he whispered quietly, not wanting to draw Mandy's attention.

He was still airily watching the outside world go by when he heard Steve call him. He turned his head towards him, "Yes?" he relied pleasantly.

Steve looked at the young lad, and considered his words before he spoke, "I wanted to thank you for last night, you probably saved my life!", his voice still nothing more than a whisper. He paused again, "Let's keep it as our secret though, I don't want you to get in any trouble", he added.

Kase nodded, smiling gently.

Steve wasn't convinced he understood how serious it could be if people found out what he had done, "Do you still have the screwdriver, or did you get rid of it?"

"I have it here" he whispered back.

"Right, give it here, I'll get rid of it for you! and if anyone asks Kase, you were in the shelter all night, yes?", he whispered again more forcefully.

He nodded again handing over the sharp tool, "Yes, all night" Kase finally replied quietly. He gave off another light smile and returned to look out the window.

It was not a long journey to their destination, pulling up at the entrance within fifteen minutes. Mandy handed money over to the driver and stepped around to the side door. She slid it open and held his hand to help his balance, leading him gently forwards into the building.

She helped Steve onto a chair, instructed Kase to stay with him and strode off to the reception counter to check him in.

***

Steve was laying on a gurney in a small treatment room of the hospital. A petite young nurse was busy stitching up a rather deep looking gash on his arm.

Mandy sat on a chair across the room, observing him carefully, she had barely spoken two words since they arrived. Her face was pale and eyes sombre.

"There we go, all done!" The nurse declared as she applied an adhesive dressing on top of the stiches.

"Thanks", Steve managed through gritted teeth, he was glad the procedure was over.

The nurse smiled, cleared up her supplies into a biohazard bin and excused herself from the room, "A doctor will be with you shortly", she said cheerily before closing the door.

"That wasn't too bad", he moaned, looking to Mandy.

She made a non-committal sound, "mhm", smiling briefly before her face returned to its stoic, glazed demeanour.

He was going to try again but the door swung open as a middle-aged man walked in. He was bald with a neatly trimmed moustache, hiding his bland features. He was dressed professionally in a light blue shirt tucked neatly into smart black trousers with a clipboard held loosely in his right hand. His demeanour exuded calmness and experience.

He pulled his chair next to the gurney and introduced himself before he sat down. He remained silent for a moment as he flicked through the pages attached to the clipboard. His brows furrowed as he read, momentarily pausing before flicking to the next page.

"Good news Steve" he declared heartily, "we have lots of surface cuts and bruises, but no breaks or serious trauma".

"So, he's OK" Mandy called out, her voice bursting with relief.

The doctor chuckled slightly, turning towards her, "No marathons for a few weeks, not until those bruised ribs heal up, but yes he will be fine" he stood up and moved the chair back to the desk.

Steve felt relief wash over him, he was almost convinced he wouldn't have a clean bill of health, not after that beating. "Thank you so much doctor".

"Yes, thanks doc" Mandy chimed in.

Steve got himself down off the table and walked over to the door, holding out his hand to the doctor.

He gladly extended his own hand bidding him fare-well, "You're free to fight another day", he said re-leasing his hand and opening the door for them to leave.

As Mandy joined him in the hallway Steve had a thought, he turned back to the doctor, "Sorry, I just wanted to ask, is there anywhere I can clean up?"

He nodded, "Of course", pointing to a room at the end of the hallway, "That is a lockable bathroom with a large sink, feel free to freshen up". With that he turned back into the room and closed the door.

Steve started walking to the room, "I will meet you in the reception babe", he turned to see her watching him closely, "I just want to clean up a little".

Mandy's face was still quite blank, she had a very pale colour since she saw him this morning. He was starting to worry but she smiled quickly, changing her features slightly, "Yes, I'll wait in reception, don't rush".

He hobbled forward into the unoccupied room; it was a large, white, tiled room. It was a spacious bathroom, a toilet surrounded with handles and support beams stood at the back wall. The sink was oversized against the wall below a ceiling height mirror.

He turned and locked the door, feeling safe for the first time since leaving the bar. He became a little upset, tears silently forming at his eyes. He refused to give into self-pity, into misery. He quickly wiped away the moisture that had formed at his eyes and tried to shake off the macabre sensation.

He delicately peeled off his clothes until he was standing naked in front of the mirror. His eyes looked down his body, suddenly he felt his stomach turn and he rushed to the toilet and vomited bile into the water.

Grabbing some tissue, he wiped his mouth and pulled the flush, washing away the vile liquid. He stood back up and cast his eyes over his body again. His chest was covered in violent purple and orange bruises. His ribs were highlighted and splattered with yet more bruises. His arms had cuts, some of which had been covered in sterile, white dressings.

Turning to the side, the right side of his bottom was again awash with an obscene purple bruise. His legs had yet more scratches and bruising on his thigh. Scanning back up his body, he leaned into the mirror. He wanted to take a closer look at his face, his nose was not broken after all, but was peppered with blood, crusted around each nostril. His lip was split, and his eyebrow had tight stiches holding the skin together.

He ran the hot water and picked up the discarded undershirt from the floor and put it on the counter. He looked for a plug but to no avail, he thought for a moment before balling up one of his socks and pushing it forcefully into the hole at the bottom of the sink.

He picked up the shirt from the counter and pumped soap into the fabric, dipping it gently into the water. Using the fabric, he washed every inch of his body gently, grimacing through the pain. The water had turned a sickening maroon colour by the time he was done.

Refreshing the water, he pumped more soap into his hand and washed his hair, finally he felt human again. He pulled out a large strip of hand towels and dried off with it as best he could, making sure to discard them into the provided bin.

Clean and mostly dry he stood naked, surrounded by the piss-stained, blood encrusted clothes. He looked again in the mirror and felt a little relieved, the bruises were still obscene, but the cuts and scratches had almost vanished, nothing more than a map of crusty red lines marking his body.

He binned the socks and white undershirt he used to wash himself, cleaned the sink off, and pulled out a plastic bag from the backpack in which to package the clothes on the floor. Thankfully, the backpack had proven to be mostly waterproof as all the clothes inside still smelt clean and felt dry. He retrieved something to wear out of the bag, "Thank you Henry, we can never repay you" he thought to himself.

Dressed and clean in fresh clothes, he almost looked as if the events of the prior night had not occurred at all, the only visible evidence, being a little stich in his eyebrow. As he painfully bent down to tie his shoes, he picked up the satchel and unlocked the room.

Slowly he hobbled down the corridor, returning to the reception where Mandy and Kase were waiting for him. As he reached the last room a sound made him stop. "BITCH! that fucking hurts" a man's voice screamed.

Steve's blood ran cold, surely it couldn't be, what are the odds. He peered into the room; the door to the chamber had been left ajar. A nurse sat next a shirtless man, he was laid on a gurney like Steve had been, this man however was handcuffed to the rail of the bed. He jolted again as the nurse worked, his eyes locked with Steve.

Anger flashed in his eyes and he turned his head away from Steve, "Wait, was it anger? No, it looked more like fear!", he thought smiling.

He felt truly renewed as he walked into the reception, even the pain seemed duller than before. Kase jumped up excitedly when he saw Steve, his face twisted into a welcoming smile, he seemed impressed at the visible change, in him. Mandy looked up from the floor when Kase moved, her features still pained, she almost looked as if she was having a painful internal battle.

He walked over to them, back to his cheery self, "That was a waste of five hours", he said magnanimously. Mandy picked up her bags and stood up, Kase held the now empty guitar case as Steve walked out the doors into the daylight, the others in tow.

"So, what's the plan?" he asked, turning to face them.

Mandy looked towards Steve then back to Kase, "Kase, just do us a favour will you, give me and Steve a moment will you?".

"OK" he replied cheerily as he walked off ahead, Mandy watched him as he continued for a few meters, out of earshot before stopping.

She motioned to the bench behind them lowering herself onto the wooden planks.

Steve sat down carefully, trying not to exacerbate any of his pain, "Are you alright Mand?".

"I can't do this again Steve". She blurted out staring at the ground. She couldn't bring herself to look at him.

His heart dropped, "No, come on Mandy, when was

the last time something like this happened?".

"That's not the point Steve, you're not a young man anymore.", tears had formed and were lipping down her face to the sun-stained concrete below. "The next time this happens, the piss head might be stronger, harder.", she sobbed. "They're going to kill you, and I can't watch you die. I can't wait for you to turn up one morning then find you dead in a gutter, or worse, never find you."

"But it's not my fault baby". He begged, reaching out a hand to try and comfort her, resting it on her shoulder.

"I know baby", she looked at him too with tear-streaked eyes. "Life on the fucking streets still, at our age it's just fucking pathetic". It was all she could do to not sob uncontrollably; she knew she had to keep it together.

"NO, Mandy, Please, we can get through this if we have each other." He pleaded, close to tears now himself.

"I can't do it anymore, I won't do it anymore, I love you so much and I'm sorry" she opened a zip in her bag and pulled out all their money, she tried to hand it to Steve, but he did not move.

She jumped up and grabbed his backpack, throwing the money inside. "Use this to get a B&B, it should be enough for a few weeks, get off the streets and claim benefits." She was on the verge of hysterical now, she knew she had to calm down. She wiped her eyes, "Promise me you will get off the streets Steve! Look after yourself".

Steve had tears streaming from his beautiful, kind eyes, "Mandy I need you, where are you going?"

"I've got to get Kase to an appointment then I'm done, I can't live like this anymore", she said wiping her eyes, "I'm done".

Steve made to stand up, but she rested a hand on his shoulder to halt him, "Don't follow me Steve, please, I couldn't just disappear and leave you with no closure. Know that I love you, please let that be enough".

She spun on her heels and walked off towards Kase briskly.

Steve was broken, what did she mean 'I'm done' "MANDY! MANDY!", he screamed, rushing to his feet. They were already quite far ahead; he didn't even bother to pick up his backpack before he tried to rush after her.

As he tried to force his leg forwards it tangled with a strap from the bag and caused him to trip. They had already disappeared from sight, they were lost, he was alone. He just lay there, tears rolling to the ground, he wanted existence to stop. How could he go on without her, his Mandy?

CHAPTER TWELVE

Mandy walked swiftly down the street. "Come on", she muttered as she passed Kase.

He sprang into action and started to follow her, "Where's Steve?" he asked, rushing to keep up with her.

She brought a hand up to her eye and discretely wiped away another stray tear, "He is going to stay here for a little bit", she lied.

"Isn't he ok now?", he asked, slowing a little, clearly torn about leaving him behind.

"it's OK hon, we have that appointment to get to though, so we have to hurry." She turned and grabbed his hand.

Reluctantly, he followed.

Mandy glanced back and saw Steve was lying on the floor, she wanted to go back but when he moved, she manged to fight the urge. She knew she had to let him be free, another tie severed.

Kase was a responsibility that she never asked for but, now she found him, she had to look out for him, he needed her. He was the last loose end, then she was truly free, free to end it all.

It took them just under an hour to walk back to the Shelter, it was approaching 4pm, the sun starting to dip in the sky. The cool breeze was refreshing against her face, she hadn't previously allowed herself to concern herself with these small wonders.

Kase remained quiet for the rest of the journey, his face was stoic, but Mandy couldn't help but notice he was enduring his own internal struggle.

The pair turned the corner and there was already a queue, "Shit!" she thought. Would they get inside in time for their meeting? She could not afford to fuck this up for Kase, this was his chance.

"Let's get in the queue quickly" she muttered hurriedly, quickly leading him towards the end.

"Mandy?" a voice called out, "I'm over here" they added.

She looked around, attempting to see the source of the words in the crowd. Suddenly Kase pointed to a woman who stood by the entrance. Her flowered dress suddenly sparking a memory, it was Gloria. "Oh hello!" she called over, swiftly walking to her.

"I wanted to meet you out here, so you didn't have to queue up, come on through" she greeted them both warmly, smiling as she spoke.

She beckoned Mandy and Kase to follow them through the entrance, some of the on-lookers had disdainful expressions. Mandy was sure she also heard some quiet whispers from them expressing their displeasure.

They walked through the security stationed at the entrance with nothing but a nod. Gloria marched straight past the bag search table and turned towards the two small offices. Mandy and Kase dutifully followed.

"Where the fuck do you think you're going?!" the man behind the baggage search table called out.

This stopped them in their tracks, Mandy was a little taken aback but started to try and explain, they were there for a meeting, after all she didn't intend to spend one more night there, or anywhere.

As soon as she opened her mouth to speak the man spoke again. "I'm not interested in your bullshit *love*. you need to wait your turn. I'm in half a mind to kick you out, fucking scum".

Mandy saw red, she took a deep breath before smiling sweetly, "Well sir, you have one thing right, you are certainly of half a mind!" she would usually have Steve there, to pull her down from her lofty rage. She free of restriction now, pausing she added, "and don't call me love. I do not need another fat, old, baldie bastard, talking down to me. Now I'm not here to stay, I'm here for a meeting with Gloria, so if you don't mind..." she batted her eyelashes and sweetened her voice, "get the fuck out of my way, *love*".

His face was contorted with anger, the woman he stood with behind the desk laughed heartily, "and that's what you get for being a dick, Jim".

He looked between them both before storming off towards the back of the hall, the woman pointed to the far office, barely managing to speak between her hysterical laughter, "she's over there".

Mandy nodded and led Kase off, a smile growing powerfully on her face.

Gloria welcomed them to the small office. It was a basic room, a desk in the middle and a scattering of chairs around it. The only thing on the desk was a battered phone and a little pot holding pens. There was a tiny window in the room and although it was too high to see out of it, it did permit the sun's rays to flood in through the open blinds.

"What was all that about?" Gloria asked, chuckling slightly.

Mandy spluttered, crashing back to reality, will she

still be willing to help Kase after the scene she just created? "I'm sorry, he was…"

"Nonsense" Gloria interrupted her, "It was brilliant, he always makes me feel uncomfortable, it was nice to see him put in his place" she added, motioning to a seat. "Right, do you want a tea before we start?" she asked kindly.

Kase and Mandy both nodded enthusiastically causing Gloria to smile and walk out of the room.

Kase looked at Mandy, eyes falling to the floor, she could see the sadness more visible now. "Why have you brought me here Mandy" he asked solemnly.

She pulled her chair closer to face him and inhaled deeply, "Look, me and Steve were on the streets for years, before that we had a home, a life, a family. I'm hoping that she can help you get that again".

He looked up, horror on his face, "No, please, don't try make me go back, I won't". He was shifting in his seat looking towards the door.

"No no no, honey it's not like that. You wouldn't be going to someone else's house; I'm trying to make them get you a place of your own. Somewhere that you can be safe, warm, free. You saw what happened to Steve last night, that's not a life!".

He calmed down slightly, eyes still darting to the door, almost planning his escape route, "You mean, in this place adults wouldn't hurt me?".

The pained way he spoke broke Mandy anew, "No sweetheart, it would be your house, only people you want in there would be allowed in as your guests". She raised her hand to wipe away the tear that had appeared on his eye, leaning in and cuddling him.

Gloria walked in mid embrace, she was holding three mugs that she placed on the desk, "Everyone OK in here?" she asked slightly concerned.

Mandy and Kase released each other, "Yes, Kase was just worried about being in the foster system again, he was ready to run away I think", she chuckled trying to lighten the mood.

"Kase", the Doctor called out, he ignored her, she repeated her call. Kase turned toward her this time "you are safe here; have you been hurt before?" He shuddered and turned back to look at the floor.

Gloria looked to Mandy and she just shrugged. Seeing she was going to get nowhere she tried a different tactic, "OK then, here's your teas", moving the mugs by each of them before taking a seat.

Seated she took a sip of her drink and placed it back on the desk, "So, I have spoken with a friend of mine, he owed me a favour. He is a social worker and I think he has secured a flat for Kase right away. I was hoping for sheltered accommodation, but he said the waiting list is too long so council accommodation it is."

"Thanks doc, that's great news, isn't it Kase?", he didn't look up.

"Please, Gloria" she corrected. She took another swig of tea and looked back to Mandy, "There are just loads of paperwork to fill out, Martin, my friend, has it with him, he should be here shortly." She said glancing at her watch.

They sat there for a little as time ticked on, Gloria started to become restless, "He's late" she declared, picking up the handset and dialling a number, "he better not have forgotten!" she mumbled scornfully under her breath.

Mandy could hear the phone ringing against her ear, a sombre feeling growing in her stomach, this all sounded too good to be true.

Her thoughts were rudely interrupted by the sound of the door swinging open loudly, a man holding a briefcase came bowling through. He slammed the door carelessly behind him. He stood for a moment, raising his briefcase up to his face and sliding his black framed gasses back on his nose.

"Hi Gloria, sorry I'm late" he called out, walking towards the desk.

She put the phone down and stood to greet him, embracing him loosely before gesturing to an empty chair. "Nice of you to join us" she quipped, smiling.

He laughed awkwardly before lowering himself into a seat. "So, is this the young man you called me about? Kase?"

Gloria exhaled deeply before she spoke, "Don't ask stupid questions Martin, I have sung your praises, don't prove me wrong". She spoke harshly but her face was jovial, her lips curved into a warm smile.

He laughed too, holding up his hand in acknowledgment, "OK, now I have some paperwork that needs completing, should we have a look at it here or should we get to the flat and do it there?"

Mandy was going to speak up, she wanted to make sure the forms were completed before she left but Gloria spoke out first. "Let's get to the flat, they may need the room before long."

Mandy was dismayed, but Martin had already stood up, "Sir, ladies, follow me to my car, I'll drive us all there.

"Yes, Mandy I forgot to ask, would you come get Kase settled in, help with his paperwork". Gloria asked warmly, giving her no real chance to refuse.

Her plans could wait another hour she thought, "Why not?", she replied standing and guiding Kase out the building and towards his car.

***

The car had driven for less than twenty minutes before it pulled up to a residential cul-de-sac on the outskirts of the city limits. There were multiple street houses lining the road with unkempt grass verges leading to rough, uneven pavements. There were trees lining the street which were overgrown but still lent an air of beauty.

They were parked in the middle of the street, looking at the rows of old, outdated but well-maintained houses. Each house was pebble-dashed, lending a pale beige, stone hue to the asphalt. There were children playing on bicycles down the far end of the road, shouting joyfully.

Martin led the way to the front door of the smaller house on their right, he produced a key from his pocket and inserted it into the lock. Mandy was looking at the building awestruck, the double-glazed bay windows poked out into the garden, shielding a little patch of grass from the scorching mid-day sun.

Mandy linked arms with Kase, "it's exciting isn't it" she said trying to liven him up, he still seemed un-responsive.

Martin swung the door open and stepped to the side, "Come on through young man" he said as he theatrically motioned.

Kase was pushed through by Mandy who followed him closely behind. The décor was bright and welcoming, the furniture was a little basic but clean and modern. Kase was looking around, sofa, television, dining table, kitchen.

Martin and Gloria joined them inside, "It's not much but it has the basics and its yours".

Mandy couldn't take her eyes off Kase, she knew something was wrong, "What's up? Aren't you happy to have your own place now?".

He remained silent, looking blandly around the room.

"Don't make me repeat myself now, you're being rude to these nice people, they have gone through a lot to sort this out for you" she scolded, her anger again escaping.

He looked at Gloria and Martin "Thank you" he said before turning to leave the room, walking towards the front door.

Mandy rushed forwards and grabbed his arm, "Talk to me" she demanded.

"The house is fine, but I can't live here" he muttered defeatedly.

Everybody in the room gasped, their faces dropped, Gloria and Martin were spluttering but Mandy kept her senses. She paused for a moment before asking why? She was gentle but forceful as she spoke, refusing to let go of his arm lest he run off before explaining himself.

He sighed and tried to compose himself, tears again forming in his eyes. "I've never lived alone, I don't have any money, I don't know how to pay bills, buy food, cook." Tears now rolling down his face, "I can't even read or write, I don't deserve this".

Mandy was deeply saddened by his words, now close to tears herself. Hearing how little he thought of himself cut her deeply, he was so young, he had seen so much and had given up on himself already. She could not find the words to reassure him, or to tell him it would be OK. She released his arm and grabbed him into a tight embrace.

Gloria broke the silence, "But Kase, that is why Mandy is here, she is going to be your caretaker. She will help you do all those things, and she will live here with you".

Martin joined in, "That's what this paperwork is about. Now you have an address, you can both make a claim for benefits. It's not a going to be a lot of money, but it will get you by."

Mandy was just about to tell Kase that it was OK, and that they had thought of everything when their words permeated her mind. "WAIT, WHAT?" she yelled wildly.

"Yes, I wanted to make sure I got you some-where safe too, you clearly care for the lad, this way you are both safe, you both have a fighting chance" Gloria replied.

Mandy collapsed to the ground, tears bursting from her, sobbing hysterically. She had been so sure. She was finally ready to end it all. She was finally ready to die. Now a chance for the new start she had chased for years is handed to her.

Kase walked to her "Mandy, are you alright?".

She was crying so much that she was simply unable to respond, joy and relief had risen upon her. She was floating in the rafters, in that moment every-thing was finally good, she couldn't wait to tell Steve.

Steve! She crashed down from the rafters leaving the elation behind. She scrambled to her feet and ran back to the bathroom, barely making it before she vomited. How could she forget? What had she done to Steve? She broke him! Her body shook, she needed to find him.

She only ended it to free him, they could have all been safe tonight, if only she had not acted so rashly. It was her fault. Yet again she ruined them, she had to put it right.

Gloria walked over and helped her up from a heap before the toilet , "Are you alright dear?".

Mandy flung her arms around her and cried into her shoulder, tears a mixture of guilt, abject despair, joy and euphoria. It took her several minutes to calm down.

She stepped back, and composed herself, "I'm OK" she insisted, "it was just a lot to hear, you have changed all of our lives". Gloria smiled kindly, eyes welling up at her reaction. She took her hand and led her back to the kitchen.

When Kase saw Mandy was ok he timidly asked, "You're going to stay with me here?".

She could not speak so she nodded earnestly causing him to burst into the biggest smile she had ever seen him muster. The whole room was lighter for it. Martin gave them a few minutes before insisting they complete the paperwork he had in a sealed portfolio within his briefcase.

It took quite a while to complete the forms with Kase, Mandy having to read questions and write his reply for him, sometimes rephrasing things in a way he understood.

Martin and Gloria were both patient and waited dutifully.

When everything was completed, Martin handed over two golden keys from his pocket "it will take a few days for me to process this but to tide you over I have filled the fridge and cupboard with some essentials".

Mandy hugged them tightly, "You saved his life you know, and mine" she whispered to them both with a final "thank you".

Kase was hungrily taking in everything he could, looking at every square inch of the building. He was even opening kitchen drawers and cupboards like he had never seen them before.

Gloria and Martin walked to the door, with Mandy following closely in tow. She was filled with a nervous energy, almost vibrating.

Gloria turned to her on the doorstep as Martin walked off to the car, "I've left my phone number in case you need anything, now, both of you, take care," she cooed.

Mandy gave her a final hug and she walked off to the car and watched as it left the road and disappeared off into the traffic.

It was gone 9pm, but she could not wait a minute more. "Kase, we need to find Steve" she called out to the house.

Kase swiftly ran back to the kitchen to join her, "isn't he in the hospital?" he asked.

"I'm not so sure, I think he would have gone

back to the shelter to look for us. It will be closed now so I'm going to have an early night and arrive before it opens, if not I will walk to the hospital."

"Can I come with you?" he asked shyly.

"Of course, sweetheart" she replied, "but I must find him, I MUST find him Kase" she was again close to tears.

Kase smiled optimistically, "We **will** find him!".

CHAPTER
TWELVE

S teve was on the ground, he was reaching out, trying to reach across space and time to Mandy. He was sobbing, a dark cloud encompassing his entire being. A nurse rushed out of the hospital entrance over to him, "Sir, are you alright?" He struggled to his knees, "She's gone!" is all he could manage.

She bent down to him and paced a hand on his back, gently trying to re-assure him, "Come on back inside, I can find someone for you to talk to", she was warm and caring in the way she spoke.

Steve shook his head, vehemently declining her offer. She offered a hand to help him to his feet, which he begrudgingly accepted. She produced a tissue from her pocket and offered it forwards, "I'm sorry for your loss", she mumbled, before turning and walking back inside.

Steve did not have the chance to explain she wasn't dead, it was worse than that, she had given up on him.

He dried his eyes with the tissue and stood, stunned, unsure of where to go, what to do. He picked up his belongings and started hobbling away, his destination unknown.

He felt numb, his stomach sick, his mind blank.

He didn't know how long he walked, the sun was still high above him lighting him with its warming rays, rays that couldn't permeate the inner coldness he felt. A sound drew him of his daze, it was an explosion of glass shattering, steel grinding on steel. He looked around and found he was in an industrial estate. The noise was coming from a recycling centre, further down this path.

He followed the path down until the road opened into a large carpark. There were rows of skips to the left, cars parked unloading into them. To the right was a chain-link fence terminating in an open gate, wide enough for industrial vehicles to easily drive through. Behind the gate was a scrapyard and recycling centre. Heaps of junk dotted as far as the eye could see. There were car pars, electronics, white goods and broken household furniture.

Steve was fascinated, feeling slightly distracted for the first time. He walked in through the gate and started to rummage the stacks of rubbish. As he was looking, he heard a voice, "How ya going? Is there anything I can help you with sir?"

The man had an American accent, filed with warmth. He was wearing a Hi-Viz jacket over a black t-shirt and dirty blue dungarees. He was around Steve's age made to look a little older by his long dirty white and grey beard.

"I'm just looking, thanks" he replied blankly.

"Is there anything you're particularly looking for; I may be able to point you in the right direction?"

"I'm just looking" he repeated, already looking back to the stacks of discarded items.

The man was patient but was a little taken aback, most people just wanted to get what they needed and get out. He could remember thousands of examples where people had demanded obscure gaskets and pipes from specific devices or cars, expecting it to be provided instantly.

"Well, if you give me a clue, I might be able to help you" he pressed on delicately.

"No just looking" he repeated yet again.

The man chuckled lightly and nodded, "Well give us a shout if you want a hand," he called as he walked away.

Steve kept looking at the stacks of waste. He had

started to collect a few pieces from the rubbish; a chopping board, copper pipe, screws, bolts, and part of a wooden stool. He was now becoming more frantic in his search, "That's not it" he kept repeating as he picked up and subsequently discarded item after item.

It had been a few hours since Steve arrived at the recycling centre, yet he was still searching. He didn't know what it was he was looking for, but he would know when he saw it.

"You found anything you want my mate?" a voice called out behind him. It was the bearded man that spoke to him before.

"I've got those" he pointed at the small gathering of junk on the floor by his feet.

"Well, what are you going to make out of all of that junk?" he asked, genuine interest in his voice.

"I still need something" he replied compulsively.

"Don't be much longer, it's nearly closing time and we've all got homes to get back to" he said turning to leave.

"You might have!" he muttered pointedly.

The man turned back to him looking perplexed for a moment before the realisation hit him. His eyes looked to the floor, a small feeling of shame burning in his throat.

"Look man, I didn't mean anything by it why don't you come and have a cup of tea in the office with me, I think I have half a sandwich from lunch I didn't eat if you want it", he offered kindly.

"No, I'm fine" Steve replied blankly.

The man was a little taken aback, "Come on, you've been out here most of the day, it's cold and I haven't seen you eat anything".

Steve stopped for a moment, he turned to face the bloke, looking at him properly for the first time. He had kind eyes nestled under a John Deere cap, shielding his face from the harsh sun's rays.

"Have I really been here that long?" he asked timidly.

The man nodded smiling.

"Now you mention it, I am a little peckish and a cuppa would go down a right treat." Steve admitted.

"Come then, it's just over there", he motioned, "Do you need a hand?"

Steve shook his head declining his assistance, and the bloke turned to walk off. He stopped at a blue container unit and waited for him to catch up. He was carrying the bits and pieces he had gathered. The man held the door open for Steve and motioned for him to enter. It was not spacious, but it had a couple of old office chairs and a table which had seen better days.

Against the back of the unit was a low fridge next to a sink. There was an old electric kettle on the fridge surrounded by dirty mugs. The man filled the kettle and rinsed two mugs as it boiled. "How do you take it?" he asked.

Steve placed the bits he found on the table and took a seat, "Milk and two please".

As the man was waiting for the kettle, he looked over the items he had gathered, "So what else is it that you're looking for?" he asked curiously.

"I don't know" he paused and pondered for a moment before continuing "a something" he replied.

"Well, I don't know what you're looking for, but I don't think there's a lot you can make out of that old junk there mate" the man chuckled heartily.

"Well could do with something metal, quite thick, ideally flat, I couldn't find anything though".

The man picked up the kettle that had finished boiling away adding milk and sugar to both cups. "What like a frying pan?".

He took the cup from the man, "Yes, that could work, I think".

He sat down next to Steve. "Kitchen stuff usually

goes into the skips at the front to be crushed, sorry".

Steve took a sip of tea and nodded, as he did a ray of light caught his eye. It wasn't coming from the door or the sky, it was coming from the floor. "What's that under there?".

The bloke exhaled loudly, "I've told them all to stop storing stuff in here". He bent down and pulled out a box "nobody bloody listens" he chuckled. In the box was a round rusty metallic object in it. "AH! think it's a hubcap".

Steve was mesmerised, it was conical and slightly raised, there were perforations around the lower side and a flat metal rim. The rust was dotted around the top and some of the perforations however, it was structurally undamaged.

"Never seen one like that before", he couldn't take his eyes off it.

"Yeah, looks like it's one from back home" he smiled.

"May I have a look?" he asked hungrily.

He nodded and handed the object to him which Steve eagerly accepted. He turned the hubcap in his hand and tapped it, listening closely to the reverberations it made. "This is it; this is what I've been looking for!" he declared excitedly, "May I have it?"

"Well friend, it's not really mine to give away, let

me find out who it belongs to" he made to walk out but he remembered something, he retrieved half of a sandwich in a foil wrapper and handed it to Steve before walking out the room.

Steve took a bite of the sandwich, from outside he heard him called "OI, Jon", he was not far away from the door.

"What", he shouted, getting no reply he shouted again, "Mark what do you want?".

"Come here!" he demanded,

"Why, what do you want?" he asked, still stacking microwaves on a pallet.

"Just fucking get here!"

Jon came jogging over to Mark, "what?" he muttered exasperated.

"Was that your thing under the desk", Mark asked.

Jon gave him a quizzical look, "That old school hubcap?" he asked. "Well, you said if I found something I wanted, I should show you first".

Mark laughed, "I also remember asking everyone to stop putting shit in the trailer". He motioned to the blue building, so it is yours?"

"Kind of", he replied. "Why, am I in trouble?" he asked nervously.

"Nah, it's just I have a guy that wants it".

"Oh, how much is he offering?" he asked, his

eyebrows slightly furrowed.

"Nothing" he said, he mouthed silently "He's homeless".

Jon looked confused, he didn't understand what Mike had tried to tell him, why he wanted to give away his hubcap for free.

Mike mouthed it again, trying to get Jon to understand, his expression remained confused. Jon shrugged his shoulders in indifference, "I want it".

Mike was getting annoyed, he was sure Jon was being purposefully difficult, "He's homeless, you nob".

Jon laughed smugly, "I might as well have it then, it's not like it's going to a good home is it".

Steve came out of the office, "Your tea went cold, I made you a fresh one " he said warmly, "also I can pay for it if that helps!", he said, reaching into his bag and pulling out the few hundred quid Mandy had left him with.

"Thanks man, we will be with you in a moment" he called out.

Steve ducked back into the office to wait for them.

"Look Jon, I'm giving it to him", he said, turning to walk back into the office.

Jon protested and went to follow him, "You're not, I'm getting it back" he insisted as he started to jog behind, following him to the office. Jon barged past Mark and started to speak hurriedly, "Look mate, I'm really…"

Steve interrupted him, "Do you take sugar?" he asked.

Jon spluttered a little, "Oh, just milk for me mate".

Steve smiled, picking up the mug and handing it to Jon. "Sorry, I interrupted you, what was you saying?"

Jon looks at him, a fresh pang of guilt hit his chest, he hesitated before he spoke. "Nothing, just that I hope you enjoy your new hubcap". He exhaled and took a sip of his tea.

Steve was excited, "Thank you, does that mean I can have it? How much is it?" he asked nervously.

Mike smiled, "No, it's yours! no charge!"

Steve was overjoyed, "This is it, exactly what I needed!" he declared.

Jon shook his head disapprovingly and stormed out mug in hand.

Steve was eagerly packing the bits he could fit into his backpack; he was just left holding the wooden plank from the stool. "Thanks for the cuppa boys, I must be off. If I'm too late I won't get a place in the shelter".

Mike looked a little saddened, "Where are you staying?"

"The shelter in the city" Steve replied still eagerly looking at the backpack containing the hubcap.

"It's quite a way" he pondered aloud, thinking for a moment, "I'll tell you what, I lock up shortly, I'll drop you down in the van if you want".

Steve looked at him and considered his generous offer, "that's very good of you sir, if that's not a burden I would be very grateful". He picked up his mug of tea and clinked it with Mark'.

CHAPTER
THIRTEEN

The journey took a little while in the dirty old van, the sun was setting in the clear sky. Eventually, the vehicle pulled up outside the homeless shelter on the curb. "There you go friend". Steve did not realise how far he walked to the scrapyard; it would have taken him hours to walk back. "Thank you, Mark", he exclaimed, "It was a pleasure to meet you, and it's Steve by the way". He shook his hand and opened the door to step out.

"Take care Steve!" he called out the open door.

Steve closed the door and waved before walking off and turning the corner.

Steve walked into the deserted alley, the dusky sky dimly lighting the entrance. The wooden door was closed, he was too late. There was nothing for it now, he resigned himself to another night on the street. He walked further down the alley towards the bins where he waited for Mandy and Kase in the morning.

He pulled the bits from the scrapyard out of his bag and gathered them on the floor. He pulled out the screws he had found and gathered them in a neat pile. Suddenly he froze, "SHIT!" he exclaimed loudly. He forgot to get any tools, a hammer or a screwdriver his plan was ruined.

He sat there and felt the despair creeping over him again, thoughts of the loss of Mandy, his loneliness, the attack he endured. His mind fell to thinking about Mandy, was she even still alive? He saw that look in her eyes before, he knew she was trying to sever ties with him so she could end it all. "NO!" he thought, "I will find her again, I will get her back, we are meant to be!".

His thoughts then ran to Kase, "That poor lad, did she abandon him too?" he wondered. "After everything he did for me, he saved me".

Suddenly he froze, he ripped open the bag and started ripping his things out onto the floor, nothing. He started ripping at the pockets, finally he stopped. He pulled out a familiar object, a screwdriver. It was the screwdriver that he took from Kase, the one he plunged into his attacker last night. The screwdriver that saved his life was again there to save him. All was not lost after all.

He picked up his possessions and threw them back into the bag before getting to work. He screwed the hubcap onto the chopping board, fastening it tightly at twelve points around the perimeter. He tapped the top of the rusted hubcap he just mounted. He bowed his head to listen, and the sound amplified and reverberated out of the perforations.

He turned the unit over and screwed four bolts into the edge of the wooden board and the stool leg onto the back. It looked odd but he was proud of his creation so far. He screwed in another block of wood to the top of the leg and attached another four bolts to that.

He pulled out the sandpaper he had gathered and started to sand the unit down. He sanded every inch, creating a smooth and supple sheen to the wood. he paid attention to the metal work, sanding it down as best he could. He sanded into the early hours of the morning until his hand was numb with the repetitive action.

When he finished polishing, he pulled out a top from his bag and spit-shined his creation, he did this until he fell from consciousness into an uneasy slumber. It was a dreamless sleep that he didn't feel peace.

A familiar loud bang woke him from his restless

nap, the sound of heavy wood banging on metal. The shelter had opened, he hurried to hide his creation in the case that had previously held his old guitar.

He threw everything back in his bag indifferently and scarpered to his feet. There was one more thing he needed, something he would not have found at the scrapyard. Luckily, he knew where he could find it.

He saw the shop as he was walking with Kase a few days ago, it was a bit of a walk, but he was resolute. He struggled to move today, his muscles were seizing, his bones were throbbing. He moved at a snail's pace, but he wouldn't stop, he was compelled forwards.

As he limped down the road, he finally saw a large clock tower in the near distance. The rustic gothic stone building that housed the clock stood guard over the city. He got close enough to read it, 8:47.

He slowly ambled up the street and ten minutes later he arrived at his destination. A music store, he tried the door, but it was locked, he could see a woman moving around inside through the window.

He waited for a few minutes before getting impatient. Steve knocked on the door, causing her to storm over. "It's not quite nine o clock", she called through the glass, pointing at her watch.

He couldn't see it, "How long have I got?" he asked anxiously.

She looked at her wrist again, "about two minutes", before she stormed off again.

Steve exhaled exasperatedly as he begrudgingly waited the two minutes for the woman to decide to come and unlock the door.

She finally did so and barged out the door past him, dragging a sign onto the pavement. He decided not to wait for her, to come back before entering the shop and eagerly looking around. By the time she had come back into the shop, he was already at the counter waiting for her. She was a little perturbed, she enjoyed the slow morning where she could enjoy her cup of tea in peace.

She slowly shuffled towards the counter, waiting until she was fully behind the narrow glass case before she acknowledged him.

"Yes sir, what can I do for you today? she asked indifferently.

He ignored the tone in her voice, "I need stings, for a guitar".

She smiled sarcastically, "You need to be more specific; we have…".

Steve did not have time for her disrespectful, haughty tone, "High gauge, brass bronze", he interrupted.

The store manager appeared from the back room with two mugs of tea in hand, "Did I hear you right? It's going to be hard to play on them" he chuckled.

Steve nodded as he handed over a note from the backpack to the woman behind the counter.

"What is it for if I may ask" he said nodding to the guitar case on his shoulder.

The woman tried to hand him a couple of pennies change, he just waved it away, "Put it in the charity pot".

Steve lay the case on the counter and unzipped it, inside it lay a bizarre contraption. It was a guitar of sorts; it had a heavily polished ash wood fret with an umber-stained tuning key. The body was made of a perfectly round polished acacia, a metal object was mounted atop it. There was no whole in the middle rather there were lots of perforations around the edge of the mount.

It looked spectacular, certainly like nothing he had ever seen before. The manager wasn't even sure it would play. "Where did you get this?" he asked, mouth agog.

"I made it" he said proudly, "last night" he added.

The woman was disinterested in the conversation but was eagerly eyeing up the strange looking instrument. "It's beautiful" she finally managed.

"Does it play?" he asked finally.

Steve grabbed the packet of strings and ripped the top, he attached them one by one. Hooking them on the base before attaching them to the tuning board at the top, tightening the bolts to secure the strings.

He pulled out the screwdriver from his bag and kept tightening the string until each one vibrated effortlessly. He picked up the instrument and held it, admiring his handywork. He plucked away at each string and it emitted a beautiful, melodious metallic note.

The woman and the manager were both astounded. Steve picked up the screwdriver and started fiddling with the bolts at the top to perfect and tune it.

The manager momentarily disappeared down an aisle, returning with a purple paisley strap. "Here, have this on me", he said handing it over to Steve.

Steve happily accepted, and thanked him, tying the strap onto the guitar. His masterpiece was completed.

Steve put the guitar back in its case and zipped it up.

The manager thought for a moment, "You know your stuff" he said proudly. "You know if you need a job I'm hiring". He looked at him hopefully.

Steve just chuckled, "No, I'm not looking anymore" he confirmed, "Thank you though, for everything" he added warmly, with that, he left the store.

***

Steve hobbled down the road until he found a doorway to an abandoned shop. He threw his backpack into the locked entranceway and gently lowered his guitar case down to the ground. He unzipped the case and pulled out his brand-new custom instrument.

He pulled the purple strap over his shoulder and pulled out the cut-off copper pipe, slipping it over his finger.

He strummed away on the guitar, and it emitted a folksy, bluesy tone. He kept strumming and playing his soulful and mystifying sound. When he had built up a rhythm he started to sing, his voice deep and raspy was so filled with pain, with power, with loss.

People paused as they walked on by, they stood and watched him, they watched the strange instrument that emitted that comforting but sharp twang. They looked at the man that was bearing his soul. This was no cover; this was a song he held close to is heart. A song about his life and journey. He sang about the slings and arrows he bore, about the love he had for his woman, a woman he had lost.

He repeated the chorus and began a new verse, the beating, the cold, the fear. He played with his eyes closed. In that moment he was no longer a corporeal being, he was one with the universe. It was the release he needed, all the unfairness he had endured, all the judgemental glares and cruel words.

The friends, the favours, the kindnesses shone high above in his words. Steve played on.

Eventually he felt himself returning to conscious thought, he felt his soul floating back down to his body. He opened his eyes and a large crowd had gathered, they were staring at him, mouths agape. He strummed the last few twangs in lyrical silence. The crowd exploded with cheers and jubilations.

People tried to hand him money which he heartily declined. People wanted to speak to him and shake his hand. He felt quite awkward with all the attention, so he decided to play something else as a distraction, this time a cover of one of the chart songs in a folksy style. It worked and the crowd settled to a quiet murmur again.

With all the attention on him, he didn't notice that a tourist had been recording his performance. He also didn't notice the man sat in the taxi on the rank, who had gotten out of his car and joined the crowd.

His second song was coming to a close and people had already started clapping and cheering. He ended with a flourish, the attention making him blush slightly.

"STEVE!" a voice called out.

The crowd looked around to see who had shouted, as did Steve, after all nobody here knew his name. For a moment, his heart jumped, was it Kase stood at the back of the crowd watching him? would he know where Mandy went? As he looked around, the voice shouted again, it was not Kase, and his heart sank. The voice instead belonged to a young lad with an ever so faintly familiar face.

"Steve, you got a sec, I really need to talk to you!" the man said urgently, forcing his way through the crowd. "Do you remember me?" he asked excitedly.

Steve racked his mind, but he just couldn't place him.

"Dan", he offered expectantly.

Steve still was still struggling.

"Jill's son" he added.

Suddenly it all came crashing back to him. He was the lad that drove them to the city in his taxi. He lurched forward and embraced him, "It's so good to see you".

"Steve, my mam asked me to look out for you, it all kicked off when you left", he said excitedly.

"Kicked off?" he asked, sounding alarmed. "What do you mean?".

Dan laughed, "Yeah, turns out my grandad's friend knew some talent scout, he heard about your performance and he is desperate to meet you. Seeing you play, I see why".

Steve was stricken with shock, "Talent scout? what?"

The crowd was just as excited by this revelation and were hanging on to every word.

"Yeah, apparently, he knew people in the business, he mentioned you at his poker game and piqued their interest. They really want to meet you!"

"That's amazing news".

"Yeah, my mam wanted me to drive you back to the bar to meet him", he chuckled. "Oh, and your lass too, Mandy wasn't it?" he added.

Steve's face dropped suddenly, Mandy, he forgot about what had happened momentarily. "We got separated" he mumbled sombrely. "I can't go anywhere until I find her".

There was a loud horn in the background, the taxi parked behind his was boxed in by his abandoned vehicle. "SHIT!" he shouted, "Look here's my card, call me when you find her, I gotta go". He handed him a business card and ran back to his car holding his hand in the air, apologising to the vehicle behind.

Steve exhaled his negativity and turned back to the crowd that had thinned out considerably. He took a deep breath and started playing again. He played until his fingers were torn and bloody, until the sun had set, and the dusk had approached.

He took a deep breath and packaged up his guitar the best he could. His fingers struggled with the zipper. He was exhausted but he grabbed his backpack and started to limp away, back to the shelter.

He was really struggling with his aching legs from being stood for hours on end. His muscles still sore from the beating. It took him over an hour to make it back to the shelter. He was in quite a bad way as he turned the corner, the pain becoming difficult to bear.

Steve looked down the alleyway, yet again there was a large queue of people hoping to get in. He hobbled the front of the queue, trying to get one of the volunteer's attention. "Excuse me" he called out.

"To the back of the queue please!", she called out without looking up.

"Of course, I just need to know if someone is in there, Kase, he's a young lad…"

She looked up from her paperwork and scrunched her face disapprovingly, "We don't run a messaging service! NOW, get to the back or you won't be coming in here, at all".

Steve considered arguing but he thought better of it, turning and limping to the back of the queue. He struggled to stand as the queue moved slowly forwards. He swayed slightly as he reached the front, only four people stood before him now.

"SORRY EVERYONE, THAT'S IT FOR TO-NIGHT, NO MORE ROOM!", one of the volunteers shouted out to the crowd.

The people remaining in the queue all grumbled and stormed off. Steve laboured forwards as they were trying to slam the door closed. "Excuse me" he called over, trying to get their attention.

"It's full bud, sorry!" she shouted back.

"No, I know, I'm just looking for someone".

"We can't give out any information" she replied, "sorry" she added before slamming the door closed.

Crushed, he hobbled back down the alleyway to the bins again. He put his bags on the floor and tried to lower himself down to the floor. He suddenly felt a rush in his head, everything went dark as he slid down to the ground.

CHAPTER FOURTEEN

Steve's body was cold and shaking, he started to come round as dawn approaches. His head was throbbing with a headache in his temple. He tried to steady himself, but he lost consciousness again.

He felt consciousness, coming back to him. He started to feel heat from the sun beaming down on him. The pain in his head throbbed. His shoulder rocked vigorously. "What's going on?" he mumbled.

His ears were ringing, he couldn't hear anything over it. His awareness was growing, his ears were still ringing but he could almost make out a voice. It sounded like someone was talking to him through an underwater tunnel. He could just about make out what they were saying, "Steve!".

He opened his eyes, struggling to focus. He kept blinking and tried to come round, letting out a low groan.

"Steve!", he heard it again, but closer.

He tried to sit up but he was struggling, thankfully a strong hand came to rest on his shoulder, offering him the assistance he needed.

His eyes finally came into focus, he looked up at the person helping him.

It was Kase!

"Steve" he called out again.

Tears came flooding to Steve's eyes, "Kase, I've been looking for you, are you alright?" he said groggily, reaching out towards him.

"I'm here Steve" he tried to re-assure him.

"MANDY!" he shouted. "Is Mandy with you? I lost her. Is she safe?" He asked desperately.

"She's safe!" he replied, "Are you alright Steve you were unconscious?".

"I was just exhausted I think, I hadn't really slept since the attack."

Kase looked worried but Steve was coming round, sensation was returning to his body. He looked around, his guitar and backpack were still tucked down beside him. He checked over his things and thankfully nothing was missing. "Where have you been?", he asked. "I've been looking for you everywhere".

"Mandy got me a house", he replied lightly, "she lives there now too".

Steve was stunned, his mind was racing with so many questions.

"We have been looking for you since you fell over at the hospital", Kase continued. "We came here yesterday but you weren't inside. We walked to the hospital, police station, all around the town. I came here again this morning to see if you made it inside while she walks around the city.

Steve was flabbergasted, "I couldn't get in last night or the day before. I was here in the alley."

"We must have only been round the corner then" Kase declared, not grasping the steely harshness of the irony.

"Everyone is all safe then?" he asked, almost refusing to believe it.

Kase nodded happily, "Should we go home?" he asked Steve warmly.

Steve's eyes lit up and he nodded, "I have some cash so let's get a taxi".

Kase helped Steve to his feet and picked up his bags. He walked with him to the taxi rank just outside of entranceway to the shelter. They walked to the nearest car and he opened the door for Steve to get in before entering himself.

The car arrived at the cul-de-sac after a short drive. It pulled up to the middle of the road and stopped. Steve paid the taxi while Kase jumped out to help him into the house. He took Steve into the living room and lay him on the sofa. Kase covered him with a blanket and Steve drifted off into a restful slumber.

The sound of a door slamming woke Steve, he sat up sharply, he is in unfamiliar surroundings.

He looked around; he couldn't remember how he got there. Suddenly, Mandy walked into the living room. She was carrying a small bag with her that she dropped immediately when she saw him.

She burst into tears and ran towards him and embraced him. They hugged for the longest time crying into each other's arms.

"Kase found me" he said softly.

She cried in his arms and poured out her apologies and regrets. She told him how she had been searching for him, how she was in a low point and was ready to end it all. How Gloria and Kase saved her from herself.

He told her all about his day making the guitar, about running into Dan and what Jill had said. He rushed to tell her all about the talent scout that wanted to hear from him. He even told her the irony of being offered a job in the music store.

Kase joined them in the room with three cups of tea and a plate of sandwiches.

It was a good night.

THE END

EPILOGUE

Steve was filled with nerves; he was about to go on stage to play. He stood in the wings of the stage; the audience hungrily stared forward laughing along with the host. It was the first time he had been invited to perform on television. To make matters worse, it was going to be broadcast live!

It had been six months since he played for the crowd in the street. So much had changed it was almost like he was living somebody else's life. He and Mandy had written down stories, their stories from the last five years, from the last few weeks, from the people they met. The stories were winding tales of sadness and joy, of friends and foes. Steve took those stories and set them against music he wrote.

A stagehand tapped him on the shoulder, "Thirty seconds" he whispered. Steve steeled his nerves, this was the most important show of his life and he knew it. If he messed up now this could all go away!

He straightened the purple paisley strap on his guitar and rested his hand on the metal hubcap body of his instrument. The host introduced him, and the stagehand pulled the luxurious red velvet curtain back to allow him to walk through onto the stage. He felt the butterflies in his stomach, he had a bad feeling about this.

***

He flung the curtain back and stormed backstage, he sped up and ran through the fire doors, he needed to be outside. He screwed up, he knew it, anger was festering, fermenting itself into rage. He needed a release, without thinking, he pulled off his guitar and slammed it down to the ground, shattering it into mere splinters.

What now, he was back to nothing, this was his chance, his one shot to make it big. His chance to tell his story to the world through. He felt sick. It was broadcast live to the word, everyone saw him screw up.

An assistant came rushing out to find him, "Are you..." he froze. "What's going on?" he asked tenderly.

"I fucked it" Steve shouted; eyes cast down to the guitar.

"I'm sorry?" he stuttered, not quite sure what was going on. "What happened to your guitar?" he exclaimed.

Steve just looked at the shards on the floor in sombre silence.

"They loved you, sir.", he said timidity. "I've never seen anything like it". he added proudly.

Steve looked towards him, "What?".

"Yeah, they loved you, people were in a stunned silence until you left the stage, they are going wild. Are you coming back for the signoff recording in a few minutes?" he asked.

Steve felt vomit rise into his throat and regret shine on the back of his neck. He solemnly nodded and followed him back inside.

***

"Yeah, I loved that guitar too!" he said re-telling the story for the hundredth time.

Mandy chuckled, "My little hot head". She grabbed his hand and pulled it up to her face, kissing it gently.

They both chuckled and grabbed their drinks, taking a deep swig.

The table was near an open, roaring fire, sending heat into their bones. The room was plastered with pictures underneath neat wooden frames. The room was busy with people who sat around them, some eating, others just chatting and enjoying their drink.

The bar around them was alive with people, the young woman behind the bar had her brunette hair pulled back into a tight ponytail. She was busy serving, every time she caught their eye, she would wink at them.

A door behind them swung closed, Mandy smiled at the person that walked through, "Come have a seat love" she said to the young man.

Kase smiled back at her as he eased himself down into an empty chair at the table. The woman at the bar walked on over to the table holding a tray. She placed the drinks down "You all doing alright?".

Mandy smiled at her, "Yeah Jill, we are".

"Kase, why don't you try a sip of beer" Jill jibed playfully.

He shook his head, but Steve joined in "Yeah Kase, try some".

Kase shrugged and grabbed a glass, he took a sip and his face contorted, "bleh!" he shouted. "I think I'll stick to fizzy drinks."

Mandy laughed, "Jill, will you join us?".

She cocked her head back to the bar, she had time, "Yeah, go on, just the one".

"Mandy, did Henry say when he would get here?" Steve asked.

Mandy put down her drink, "Yeah, shouldn't be too long".

"I've made up your old room" Jill said to the pair, "And you, young man, have your own room made up".

Kase looked up at her "Thank you ma'am".

"So, how's the new album coming along Steve" Jill asked.

Steve smiled, "Very well" he replied. "Should be released next month, I just hope it does as well as the first!".

"Another number one? doesn't want for much does he?" Mandy jibed playfully.

Everyone at the table laughed, the mood was jovial and joyous. The bar held such warm memories for them, it felt like home. Steve's mind floated off to the day he played his guitar in the centre, the day he ran into Dan. Steve remembered the relief of Kase finding him, of the euphoric moment Mandy ran into his arms that night.

He could not have dreamt what was to come when he called Dan. He came and picked them up, bringing them to the bar. Jill put them in contact with her father's friend and the talent scout. He played for him at the bar, and he signed him on the spot to his record label.

He was given a small retainer fee, enough to be more than comfortable. As much as Mandy protested, he used most of it to buy Henry a new tractor. He chuckled remembering the arguments they had. The last year had really been a ride, thankfully they still had each other.

A voice called him back to the moment, "How do!".

"Henry, so good to see you!", Steve called out as Mandy scrambled to her feet.

She wrapped her arms around him, "It's so good to see you again!".

Henry went to the bar, "Come on lad, give me a hand" he called over to Kase. They returned with another round of drinks for everyone. Henry joined them at the table as they all reminisced.

"Where are you living now?" Henry asked.

Mandy's face twisted into a spectacular smile, "We bought a house in the country a little while ago, four bedrooms, we finally finished decorating!".

"It's beautiful, Mandy has done a bang-up

job" Steve added excitedly.

Mandy put her arm around Kase, "You're happy with your room too, aren't you?".

Jill smiled, "I thought you had a place in the city?" she asked.

"I didn't like it there all by myself, even though they took care of all the bills it was lonely, so Steve and Mandy offered to let me stay with them, they look after me now, we're a family" said Kase. Everyone looked touched at his words, his face flushed a little from the expressions on their faces.

The table all continued to relive, laugh and joke into the late hours. As the night pulled in, the bar started to empty out. The guests at the table started to feel weary and groggy. Henry got to his feet, "I'm done for tonight, do you have a room spare for me Jill?".

She nodded, "Of course Henry, always for you".

"Steve, walk me up", Henry asked.

Steve smiled and got to his feet. Henry led the way until they were out of earshot. "I wanted to tell you something Steve, Something private."

Steve put his hand on Henry's shoulder, "Anything!".

Henry took a deep breath, his expression filled with concern. He finally managed "I've had to sell the farm", he took a deep breath, "I can't keep up running it. It kills me to lose it but it's too much for me now".

Steve embraced him, he could see the pain he was

in, "You could have asked for help Henry".

Henry shook his head, "NO" he said firmly.

"Aren't you going to miss your farmhouse, all your memories" Steve asked.

Henry looked defeated; he did not know how to respond so he just shrugged.

Steve smiled warmly, "It's your home Henry", he put his hands in his pocket. "I heard that you were selling the farm already". Steve's lips were still curved into a smile, "and I had my solicitor make a little acquisition".

"What do you mean?"

Steve laughed, "I mean, I bought your farm", he paused, "bought it for you". "You can't give up your home, I know what that feels like all too well".

Henry flung his arms around Steve, tears in his eyes.

"Goodnight Henry, I'll speak to you tomorrow anyway".

Steve watched Henry walk up the stairs and turn in towards one of the rooms. He turned back and returned to the table. The bar was empty, Jill had left Mandy and Kase sitting at the table as she tidied up. Steve slid into his seat and joined the table.

They were together.

They were a family.

Printed in Great Britain
by Amazon